Playing

KATHRYN BELLAMY

Heartline
Books

KATHRYN BELLAMY

KATHRYN BELLAMY was born in Lincolnshire, one of the most beautiful cathedral cities in England, and still lives there. She was educated at Queen Elizabeth Grammar School in Horncastle, Lincolnshire and, after gaining excellent examination results, went to work in a Bank.

A number of part-time jobs followed which left Kathryn free to concentrate on what she enjoys most – writing, and *reading*, romantic fiction. Amongst her favourite authors are Jilly Cooper and Rosemary Rogers and Kathryn admits to a secret passion for bodice rippers!

In her spare time she enjoys reading, tennis and yoga. But perhaps Kathryn's most challenging pastime at the moment is going on safari to the bottom of her garden – where she never knows what she might find, as recent visitors have included snakes and giant toads!

Did you miss HIS BROTHER'S KEEPER, Kathryn Bellamy's first novel for Heartline Books? If you did, why not call the Heartline Hotline – 0845 6000 504 – and pay by credit/debit card, or send a cheque/postal order for £4.49 (including p&p), made payable to Heartline Books Limited, to us at HEARTLINE BOOKS Ltd., PO Box 400, Swindon SN2 6EJ and we'll send you the book by return.

Heartline Books –
Romance at its best

chapter one

Gina Bruce parked her car neatly alongside that belonging to her sister-in-law, Emily, and clambered out, stretching to ease her back muscles after the drive from London. Her small hatchback was ideal for city traffic and restricted parking spaces, but was definitely not the fastest or most comfortable car for the longer journey to the coast.

It would have been more sensible to have remained in Falworth overnight after the funeral, she acknowledged now, but at the time, the need to escape to her own flat had been too great for her to consider the practicalities of her action.

She stared up at the façade of the huge, red-brick house, bleak and unwelcoming even in the Spring sunshine, and made no move to enter her childhood home as she wondered once more why her father's solicitor, David Williams, had insisted on this morning's formal reading of the will.

She turned swiftly at the sound of a car horn tooting and smiled warmly at her twin, waiting while he emerged from his BMW and joined her. Gavin had the dark hair and brown eyes they had both inherited from their mother, but there the resemblance ended and there was nothing to indicate that they were twins. Gavin had none of Gina's delicate bone structure and elfin features, but was tall and broad, and ruggedly attractive in a very masculine way.

'Hi,' she greeted him. 'What's the reason for the family gathering – do you know?'

'No,' Gavin shrugged. 'David Williams was rather

cagey yesterday when I asked him about the will, God knows why. Unless Dad changed it recently, his shares in the company come to me, and the house is yours.' He paused and looked at her searchingly. 'I tried to phone you last night. I was worried about you.'

'I'm fine now,' she assured him.

'No, you're not,' he contradicted. 'Stop feeling guilty, Gina,' he admonished quietly.

'I'm not…' she began, then stopped. Lying to her twin was futile.

'Listen to me,' Gavin said urgently. 'He was a hard, cold man with no paternal feelings for us and it is not our fault that we didn't love him! He never wanted our love, just our obedience. I feel as badly as you do, Gina, but he pushed us away when we were still babies. It was his choice, not ours.'

'I know you're right,' she sighed. 'But to die, all alone…' she swallowed convulsively. It had been the housekeeper's day off when Peter Bruce had suffered his fatal heart attack, and he had lain unattended for some hours. Despite the doctor's assurance that he had probably died instantly, Gina couldn't help but wonder if he had been aware of what was happening, but been unable to summon help; if he'd had time to feel afraid…

'He died as he lived,' Gavin said harshly. 'Did you notice there was no one at the funeral who could be counted as a true friend?'

'I noticed,' Gina said sadly. 'But a lot of people did attend, more than I had expected.' She had been surprised to find the church so full.

'Yes, to pay their respects,' Gavin stressed the word. 'He was a good employer, a fair man to do business with. But no one was there to weep for him, Gina.'

'Emily cried,' Gina remembered. She had envied her

sister-in-law the release of tension and wished for similar relief from her own numb sense of shock.

'Oh, Emily,' Gavin's tone was indulgent, if somewhat exasperated. 'She always cries…' he broke off, frowning at the sight of a black Jaguar pulling into the drive. 'What the…?'

'Who is it?' Gina asked, unable to distinguish the driver through the tinted glass. 'That's not Mr Williams' car, is it?'

'No. That's Jack Dawlish!' He almost spat the words and Gina stared at him in consternation.

'Isn't he the financial advisor Dad's been consulting recently?' She tried to recall what Gavin had told her about Jack Dawlish. He was something of an economics whiz kid, a partner in a merchant bank based in London, and Gavin had fought against his involvement in their family firm in vain. 'What's he doing here?'

'That's what I'd like to know,' Gavin said grimly. 'I hope he's come to pack his bags!'

'You mean, Dad actually invited him to stay here, at the house?' Gina asked incredulously. Their father had valued his privacy, and visiting business colleagues were usually booked in at Falworth's top hotel or, since Gavin's marriage, stayed with him and Emily. 'He must have liked him a lot,' she commented.

'Yeah, he did,' Gavin agreed moodily. 'But I don't. I'll need to appoint a financial director, but it won't be Dawlish, that's for sure.' He deliberately raised his voice as he spoke, and Gina laid a restraining hand on his arm, watching keenly as the man her twin clearly hated climbed out of his car and walked towards them.

The tension emanating from Gavin was palpable, and Gina felt her own body stiffen with resentment. Prickles of unease feathered her spine and, when the sun disappeared briefly behind a cloud, she gave an involuntary shiver of apprehension. Goose pimples rose on her skin and, for some inexplicable reason, she felt that this man spelled danger! She began finding it difficult to breathe and stood rooted to the spot, still clutching Gavin's arm.

Jack Dawlish was younger than she had expected; early thirties, she guessed, but there was a stern, hard cast to his features, which belied his years. He was as tall and broad as her brother and the expensively tailored City suit only served to emphasize his powerfully muscled torso and long, lean legs. His hair was black and cut short, his eyes a cool, clear grey as they surveyed the twins. The surprisingly full mouth thinned to a disapproving line as he came to a halt in front of them.

The Terrible Twins, Jack thought grimly. Their own father had described them thus, and not with affection either. Their mother had died when they were ten-years-old and, according to Peter Bruce, they had built an invisible wall around themselves, shutting out everyone else. He could now see exactly what their father had meant, and felt a pang of sympathy for Emily, Gavin's wife. Peter Bruce had been pleased by the marriage, hoping it would break the hold Georgina had over her twin, but Emily was too mild, too lacking in confidence, too aware that Gavin was the boss's son, and had probably only offered marriage because she had become pregnant. That she had miscarried the baby only a few days after the wedding seemed to have undermined her confidence further.

'Gavin,' Jack acknowledged with a brief nod, his voice deep and well modulated. He then submitted Gina to a scrutiny that was somehow insulting in its brevity, as if she were of no account. 'You must be Georgina,' he stated, making no move to shake hands, an omission for which she was grateful while at the same time resenting his easy dismissal of her.

'Gina,' she corrected him automatically, for she hated being addressed as Georgina. She was feeling strangely dizzy and was glad of Gavin's supporting arm – or was she supporting him? She no longer knew which. 'Only my father called me Georgina – he wanted me to be a boy,' she babbled on foolishly, and then found herself blushing. Heavens! She'd not blushed in years!

'Really?' Jack Dawlish drawled, raising one sardonic eyebrow, and Gina felt more colour suffuse her cheeks. Just that one word conveyed boredom and contempt, and she knew instinctively that he considered her remark a well-rehearsed ploy; that he thought she had been fishing for a compliment, an assurance that no male could possibly wish her to be anything other than a girl.

'What are you doing here, Dawlish?' Gavin demanded rudely, and Gina was grateful for his intervention, able to breathe a little easier once the cold, grey eyes were turned in her brother's direction.

'Your father's lawyer asked me to be here,' he said mildly enough, but Gina sensed steel beneath the quietly spoken words. 'I'm sorry I missed the funeral,' he continued, 'however, *if* I had been informed…'.

'Sorry, it didn't occur to me,' Gavin said carelessly. 'Anyhow, I thought you were busy interfering in some other poor man's business this week?'

'Gavin!' Gina hissed in some alarm, noting the hardening of Jack Dawlish's mouth, the angry thrust of his jaw. But then he visibly relaxed and slowly smiled, and that somehow frightened her even more…

'You are obviously unaware that your father appointed me co-executor of his will,' he said casually and sauntered past them towards the house, then pivoted on his heel to add, 'so you can expect rather more…interference from me in the future.'

'What does that mean?' Gina tugged at Gavin's arm as he stared speechlessly after the retreating figure of his enemy.

'It means he can make life very difficult for the next few months, until the estate is settled,' Gavin explained tersely. 'What on earth was Dad playing at?' he ground out, and Gina shrugged helplessly.

'Maybe Mr Williams knows the reason?' she suggested. 'He should be here any minute,' she glanced at her watch. 'Here he is now,' she said with relief, and hurried to meet the family's solicitor with Gavin close at her heels.

'I thought you were the sole executor of Dad's will – what's this about Jack Dawlish being involved?' Gavin demanded. David Williams hesitated and stifled a sigh. He had asked Peter Bruce to tell the twins about his plans. Obviously, he hadn't considered it necessary.

'Let's go into the house, shall we?' he said quietly. Gina sensed Gavin was about to interrupt and she caught at his arm.

'Listen to what he has to say before losing your temper,' she pleaded and, after a moment, he nodded and smiled down at her reassuringly.

Emily was hovering in the hallway as they entered, her eyes seeking her husband's anxiously as if she were aware of forthcoming trouble, Gina noted. She noted, too, that Jack Dawlish murmured something to Emily in passing; a brief comment only, but one which brought a light to her eyes and a smile to her lips.

Gina narrowed her eyes suspiciously, wondering if Gavin's hostility was of a rather more personal nature than the natural rancour he had felt when their father had brought an outsider into the family firm. No, she was imagining things! Gavin would have confided in her if he felt his marriage was under threat and, besides, Emily was besotted with Gavin; she wouldn't look twice at another man, especially not Jack Dawlish. Not only was he a thorn in Gavin's side but, despite his undeniable good looks, he possessed about as much warmth and charm as a computer.

Convinced she was being over-sensitive and worrying about a problem which didn't even exist, Gina pulled her thoughts together and politely offered coffee which was declined and, at Mr Williams' suggestion, they all moved into Peter Bruce's study. The solicitor placed his briefcase on the desk and, pointedly ignoring their father's leather swivel chair, pulled up another and sat down, rifling through the papers in his case while the rest of them took their places.

Gina perched on the edge of the leather chesterfield facing the desk, with Gavin next to her and Emily on his other side. Jack Dawlish was the last to enter the room.

'Which chair do you think he'll take?' Gina whispered to her brother.

'One we can plug in to the mains hopefully,' he muttered, and she choked back a laugh. However, Jack also ignored Peter Bruce's chair and walked over to the window and leaned negligently against the wall, arms folded across his chest as he surveyed them all. He seemed more at ease than the family, Gina decided with some irritation, since she was feeling distinctly uncomfortable and she was sure Gavin shared her unease.

This room had always been their father's domain; she and Gavin had only ever been summoned here when they were in trouble – which had been fairly often, she acknowledged silently, and exchanged a wry grin of mutual understanding with her twin. She felt a sudden compulsion to glance across at Jack Dawlish and discovered that his eyes were boring into hers, a dark scowl marring his features. She looked quickly away, for some reason unable to meet his gaze, and sat twisting her hands rather nervously in her lap.

She was relieved when Jasper, the family cat, pushed his way into the study and jumped, rather stiffly due to his advanced years, up on to her lap. She began to fuss over him and he purred his pleasure, spreading his claws against her jacket. It was expensive, new, and made of very soft suede, so Gina shrugged it off before he could damage the material. Jasper snuggled up against her as she continued stroking him and Jack, watching, had three very unwelcome thoughts flash through his mind in quick succession. She isn't wearing a bra. She doesn't need to. I wish I were that cat! He forced his gaze – and his thoughts – away from her and turned his attention to David Williams, not envying him his task.

'I'll just quickly run through the smaller legacies first,' he cleared his throat and began reading. Gina only half-listened, too aware of Jack Dawlish to be able to concentrate fully. There were substantial bequests to Mary, the housekeeper, and to Miss Pettit, Peter Bruce's secretary for more than twenty years, and various sums to local charities.

The collection of antique jewellery which had belonged to Peter Bruce's mother and grandmother, was for Emily, the newest Bruce wife. She gasped with pleasure, and then looked anxiously at Gina, as if afraid she might object. Gina smiled reassuringly; she certainly didn't want the jewellery for herself and only hoped Emily wouldn't be disappointed when she saw it. From what Gina could remember of it, the pieces weren't particularly valuable or even very attractive.

Gavin nudged Gina with his elbow then, as he caught her eye, made a slight gesture with his hand, as if throwing something away. Gina nodded and bit her lip to stifle her laughter, knowing immediately to what he was referring. She clearly recalled the incident which had taken place when they were quite small, perhaps five or six-years-old. They had been in their parents' bedroom while their mother prepared for an evening out, and had witnessed an argument where Vivienne Bruce had refused point blank to wear her mother-in-law's jewellery. When their father tried to insist, Vivienne had settled the dispute by tossing the entire contents of the jewel case out of the window...

Gavin nudged her again and Gina jerked her thoughts back to the present, suddenly aware that Mr Williams had paused and was looking at her questioningly. As was Jack Dawlish, only he wasn't regarding her quite so benignly as the older man...

'Sorry, go on,' she murmured.

'This house, and its contents, go to Gavin and Gina equally, to dispose of as they wish. 'However,' he coughed and regarded them both intently, 'it was your father's wish that Mr Dawlish should continue to use "The Beeches" as his base in Falworth until such time as the estate is settled and the house is legally yours.'

'That will be our pleasure,' Gavin muttered sarcastically, glaring at Jack Dawlish. Mr Williams sighed heavily, but forbore to comment further. Jack Dawlish merely smiled slightly, acknowledging both Gavin's displeasure and his inability to do anything about it.

'The bulk of the estate, namely the seventy per cent holding in Bruce Casuals, is divided as follows. Five per cent goes to Gina, ten per cent to Gavin, which, added to the fifteen per cent they each inherited from their grandfather, gives them twenty and twenty-five per cent respectively…'

'What?' Gavin interrupted, sitting up straighter.

'The remainder goes to James Andrew Dawlish,' Mr Williams continued expressionlessly.

'There must be some mistake!' Gavin jumped to his feet, his hands balled into fists at his sides. 'That gives him fifty-five per cent – a controlling interest!' he burst out, obviously doing his sums quicker than Gina who was still struggling to comprehend the implications of what she had just heard. Their father had disinherited Gavin! That was what it amounted to! All his life he had known he was to carry on the family business; had been discouraged to even consider an alternative career – and now this…betrayal!

'No, there's no mistake,' David Williams said quietly. 'And I have to tell you now, Gavin, that your father gave Mr Dawlish Power of Attorney some weeks ago. That means he can take over the running of the company immediately, without waiting for the legal formalities to be completed.'

'Why would Dad do this?' Gina asked of no one in particular, and received no reply other than a shrug of disbelief from Gavin. She watched in bewilderment as Mr Williams took a sealed envelope from his briefcase and offered it to Jack Dawlish, who took it without comment and slipped it unopened into the inner pocket of his jacket.

This bombshell came as no surprise to him, she noted bitterly, and understood now the meaning of that slow, cruel smile he had bestowed upon them earlier. He had known then that Gavin was about to lose everything he had worked so hard for – known and revelled in his knowledge! Surely he could see that this simply wasn't fair?

'Is that a letter from our father?' Gina challenged him, gently putting the cat to one side before getting to her feet to stand by her twin. 'The least you can do is open it and tell us why he's done this to Gavin.'

'I already know his reasons,' Jack Dawlish drawled. 'And I have no intention of allowing you to read a personal letter addressed to me,' he added coldly, in the manner of an adult rebuking a child for an appalling display of bad manners.

'But...' she began hotly, only to be interrupted by Gavin.

'Forget it Gina, don't give him the satisfaction of arguing with him. But don't think you've won, Dawlish,' he warned. 'We're not taking this lying down. This is our inheritance. We deserve it!'

'Obviously your father disagreed,' Jack Dawlish said coolly, as his gaze swept over the twins; Gavin, red-faced and furious, Gina, pale, her eyes wide and dark with shock. 'I'm inclined to think you've got precisely what you deserve – both of you,' he bit out.

'We'll contest this travesty of a will!' Gavin snapped at him, but Jack Dawlish merely shrugged indifferently. 'My father's state of mind must be in doubt – handing over a controlling interest in the family business to a virtual stranger!' Gavin spluttered. Faced with Jack's bland countenance, he turned to the solicitor instead. 'Can't you do anything?' he demanded.

'As co-executor of your father's will, it is my duty to carry out his wishes,' David Williams said quietly but with some sympathy. 'And I have to tell you now, Gavin, that in my opinion, there is no doubt about your father's state of mind; he was very clear in what he wanted to do.'

'Then I'll find another solicitor!' Gavin almost snarled at him. Gina watched him fight for control of his emotions, her heart twisting with pity for him. Finally, she saw some of the tension drain from him as his shoulders sagged.

'There's no point in hanging around here,' he muttered and headed for the door. 'Are you coming?' he paused to bark at Emily, who had sat, quiet and forgotten, while he ranted. She nodded and scrambled to her feet, hurrying after her husband and avoiding looking at anyone else.

Gina grabbed her jacket, for her instinct was to follow Gavin, then she paused and remained where she was, shrugging on the jacket as if merely feeling cold. No doubt both twins leaving would give untold satisfaction to Jack Dawlish, but the house belonged to her and Gavin now and, even if they were legally bound to allow the inter-loper to stay at 'The Beeches', she wasn't inclined to give him total freedom to treat the place as if it were his own!

'I have to be on my way too,' David Williams broke the silence and began piling papers back into his briefcase. 'Unless you have any questions, Gina?' he smiled kindly. Not while Jack Dawlish is listening to every word, she thought.

'No,' she forced an answering smile, feeling quite sorry for him. It couldn't have been easy for him, coming here today knowing what news he had to impart. 'Can I get you coffee or a glass of sherry?' she offered.

'No thank you, my dear. I have a lunch appointment,' he patted her arm gently and left, with some relief, Gina thought wryly, as she closed the front door behind him.

Aware of footsteps behind her, she stiffened and slowly turned to face Jack Dawlish. She scanned his face for any sign of triumph, but his gaze was bland and impenetrable.

'Are you leaving too?' she asked hopefully, wrenching open the door and flinging it wide. 'Goodbye. I'd like to say it's been nice meeting you but...'

'Sorry to disappoint you,' he smiled thinly, 'but I'm staying a while. I'm just going to fetch my briefcase from my car. Why don't you go and make us both some of that coffee you mentioned?' he suggested. Gina opened her mouth to tell him to make his own stupid coffee, then closed it again when he added, 'we have a few matters to discuss.'

'We do?' Hope flared as he nodded and walked past her. If he was prepared to discuss the will, then perhaps he realised the unfairness of it and was willing to make amends, despite what he had said to Gavin? There was obviously a mutual dislike between the two men, so maybe he had wanted Gavin to sweat a little, she thought, feeling slightly happier as she went to the kitchen to make coffee.

She carried a tray back to the study, pausing in the doorway when she noted he was ensconced behind her father's desk looking thoroughly at home. Her lips tightened, and her optimism faded somewhat. He certainly didn't look like a man prepared to hand back an undeserved inheritance!

'Shall we go into the drawing room?' she asked coolly.

'No,' he glanced up briefly, then continued reading. 'Come and sit down, Gina.' Silently she obeyed, and busied herself pouring coffee while covertly watching him, hoping to see a sign of softening in his harsh features. There wasn't one, though she did notice how long his lashes were, fanning his cheeks as he read.

'Thanks.' He took the cup and saucer she pushed towards him and leaned back in his, or rather her father's chair, and surveyed her intently. Although Gina had resented his earlier, quick dismissal of her, she found herself feeling awkwardly self-conscious beneath this cool-eyed scrutiny that missed not one detail of her appearance.

She was accustomed to men giving her second and third glances, and knew she looked good in the suit she had chosen to wear. It was dusky pink suede and comprised a knee-length, straight skirt and fitted jacket with a matching broad belt, which cinched her narrow waist. The colour suited her creamy skin and she knew her dark hair was shining, softly framing her face, knew her make-up was immaculate, subtly emphasising the large brown eyes which were her best feature. She knew all this, yet it was suddenly of no consequence. Jack Dawlish didn't give a damn about the way she looked; he was studying her with the same impersonal attention he had been affording the papers spread before him on the desk.

'I want to return to London as soon as possible,' she said stiffly, placing her own unwanted coffee cup back on to the tray, 'so can we discuss Gavin's inheritance now?'

'Gavin's inheritance?' His brows rose in feigned surprise. 'I believe he's inherited a half-share in this house plus an additional ten per cent holding in Bruce Casuals,' he said blandly. Gina dug her nails into the palms of her hands, trying to control her temper. She failed.

'You know perfectly well what I'm talking about!' she ground out. 'The fifty-five per cent you persuaded Dad to leave to you! That belongs to Gavin! What have you ever done to deserve it?'

'Obviously, I've earned your father's trust and respect,' Jack Dawlish retorted sharply. 'Which is something neither you nor your brother succeeded in doing!'

'I'm not listening to this!' Gina jumped to her feet and turned towards the door – she must have been crazy to think he might be prepared to behave in a just and reasonable manner. Gavin's dislike and mistrust of the man were well founded.

'I won't be renewing the lease on your flat.' The quietly

spoken words stopped her in her tracks, and she spun round to face him.

'What did you say?' she demanded incredulously.

'You heard. Sit down,' he nodded towards the chair she had just vacated and Gina slowly did as he said, needing the solid support beneath her. She was visibly shaking and clenched her hands together in an attempt to conceal the betraying tremors. She licked her suddenly dry lips and determinedly squared her shoulders.

'You can't do that,' she said, but her voice wasn't as confident as she would have liked.

'Yes I can,' he contradicted. 'It's high time you faced up to the realities of life and I intend to see that you do. The bills on your flat are all paid for by the company – a luxury the business can no longer afford. And the generous allowance your father paid you no longer exists, since his bank will have frozen all transactions on his personal account,' he pointed out. This was something which hadn't even occurred to Gina, and she began to feel trapped. How was it possible that a man she hadn't even met until an hour ago could turn her life into a nightmare?

'But...but I already own fifteen per cent of the company, twenty now,' she said desperately. 'I'm a director! The flat is paid for out of my share of the profits,' she said, a small measure of confidence returning.

'What profits?' Jack drawled. 'Bruce Casuals is in a bad way financially, but I don't suppose you would know about that since your empty head is only concerned with shopping and night-clubbing,' he said contemptuously. 'Tell me, when did you last attend a board meeting?'

'When I was last invited to – which was never!' Gina flashed back. 'My father didn't approve of women in business. I acted as his hostess when he needed to entertain and that was the full extent of my duties as a director. That was the way he wanted it and you have no right to walk in and change everything!'

'Your father gave me that right,' he reminded her calmly. 'The first thing I intend to do is review the directors' fees.'

'Oh yes?' Gina looked up, her lip curling in disdain. 'How much are you going to take for yourself?' she asked bitterly, then shrank back in her chair as he leaned menacingly towards her, anger evident in the tight line around his mouth.

'I'm not taking a penny!' he rasped. 'And neither are you, unless you earn it. Tell me, what do you know about the textile industry?'

'I know a designer label when I see one!' she retorted. His eyes narrowed at her tone.

'A pity you can no longer afford to buy them,' he replied swiftly, and Gina flushed angrily. 'I repeat, what do you know about the textile industry?'

'About as much as you, probably. After all, you're only a glorified bank clerk, aren't you?' she smiled sweetly. Jack was hanging on to his temper with the greatest of difficulty. No wonder her father had found her impossible to control, he thought.

'Don't push your luck,' he warned her. 'I am rapidly running out of patience with you, young lady. We are not discussing my qualifications or achievements. We're discussing yours, which won't take long, will it?' he enquired snidely. 'You're not exactly over-qualified, are you?'

'You know nothing about me!' Gina said furiously, then her jaw dropped when he slowly pulled open his briefcase and slapped down a folder on top of the desk. A folder bearing her name.

'I have a dossier on you – not pretty reading,' he said

coldly. Gina could only stare at it dumbly as tears pricked the back of her eyes. This hateful man could only have gained his information from her father and, despite their differences over the years, it hurt unbearably that he had trusted a virtual stranger with private, family matters. She sensed he was watching closely for her reaction and forced a smile to her lips as she settled back in her chair and crossed her legs.

'It's supposed to be a red folder,' she told him conversationally. 'And you should be disguised as a hat stand or something and burst into the room, saying, "Gina Bruce! Tonight, This Is Your Life!" ' she intoned dramatically, and had the satisfaction of seeing his lips tighten in annoyance. 'What surprises do you have in store? Where have you hidden all the people from my past?' she asked gaily. 'Where are the teachers who hated me at the time but are prepared to say what a brilliant student I was, if it means they'll get their faces on television?'

'I doubt very much if any teacher unfortunate enough to have attempted to educate you would have the gall to publicly admit their failure,' Jack bit out. 'Now, have you quite finished? Or shall we continue the game? Shall I list your achievements?' he enquired silkily, and Gina wished she hadn't tried to rile him. She shook her head, but he went on remorselessly.

'Shall we start with you being expelled from boarding school?'

'I wanted to be expelled,' she tried to explain. 'Gavin and I were separated and we…'

'It had nothing to do with your brother!' Jack interrupted. 'You were kicked out for smoking, smuggling alcohol into the dormitory, and generally being disruptive in class. It was a similar story at finishing school, with the extra touch of being caught sneaking out late at night to meet up with some of the local boys!' There was utter disgust in his voice and Gina cringed.

'That was for a dare…' she protested miserably, but he cut through any explanation she might have to offer.

'You've never stayed in any job for more than a few months…' He paused to consult his wretched folder. 'Ah yes, you managed to last six weeks as an *au pair* before your employer sent you packing…'

'His wife sent me packing, as you call it, because her pig of a husband wouldn't leave me alone and she chose to believe I was at fault, not him!' Gina said bitterly. She might have known she would be wasting her breath.

'And you gave him no encouragement, I suppose?' Jack asked caustically.

'If you had seen him, you'd know you're talking rubbish!' Gina spat at him. 'He was fat and fifty! I never encouraged him at all. And I was glad to leave – the children were brats,' she added for good measure.

'You should have been on their wavelength then,' he returned swiftly. 'The word "brat" suits you to a T.'

'Who told you all this? Our father? Did he also tell you that our mother died when we were only ten-years-old? And that he separated Gavin and me when we most needed to be together? That he ignored our pleading and sent us away to boarding school because he couldn't be bothered to look after us…' She broke off, horrified to find herself almost in tears. How it still hurt though, even after all these years. She blinked rapidly and bit savagely at her lower lip to try and regain control of her emotions, hating to have Jack Dawlish witness her distress.

'Tears don't impress me, Gina,' he said coolly. 'Nor am I concerned with the past, only with what happens in the future. If you want to remain in London, you'll have to find a job.'

'I already have a job!' she snapped.

'Oh, yes, helping Sophie Allinson with her so-called catering business,' he said mockingly. 'The only people who hire her are those hoping to do business with her father; sycophants who could quite easily send out their own staff to dash around the nearest Marks and Spencer food hall for finger food and transfer it to plates...' He raised one eyebrow questioningly, as if daring her to contradict. Gina stared back, trying not to blush. They didn't resort to that, well, not often...how on earth did he know? Or was he guessing? She tilted her chin higher.

'Both Sophie and I are excellent cooks,' she said haughtily, which was true.

'I'm glad to hear it,' he didn't sound convinced. 'But do you earn enough to be self-supporting?'

'No,' Gina whispered after a long moment, well aware that the astronomically high rent on her flat was far beyond her means.

'No,' Jack repeated. 'You don't have a choice, Gina. Go back to London for the weekend, by all means, but I want you at the factory on Monday morning, nine o' clock sharp,' he said crisply. Gina glared at him, but had no answer other than a muttered 'Go to hell!' before she hurried out of the room.

chapter two

Gina was somewhat surprised – but relieved – that he allowed her to have the last word, but her triumph was short-lived. She stepped out on to the gravel drive, then gasped in outrage as she saw he had moved his car – presumably while she had prepared the coffee – and had blocked her exit!

She wrenched open the door of the Jaguar in the rather vain hope that he had been careless enough to leave the key in the ignition but, of course, he hadn't. She glared at the car in impotent fury and was contemplating aiming a kick at the gleaming paintwork when she heard the front door opening. Whirling round, she saw Jack Dawlish leaning against the wall and regarding her with undisguised amusement.

'Still here?' he enquired blandly, dangling a bunch of keys from one finger.

'What are you playing at?' Gina ground out.

'I didn't want you dashing off before I'd had the chance of spelling out your future as a working girl,' he told her, still making no move towards his car.

'Move it!' Gina snapped, and he arched one eyebrow at her tone.

'Ask nicely,' he suggested, and Gina ground her teeth in annoyance. How Gavin had resisted the temptation to flatten the wretched man, she would never know.

'Move it. Now,' she gritted out, and his mouth quirked in evident amusement.

'That's asking nicely?' he queried.

'If you don't move it this minute, I'll…' she struggled to think what she could do, short of murder, which would have been her first choice. 'I'll let the tires down!' she threatened. He laughed then, throwing back his head, evidently enjoying her predicament thoroughly.

Gina took immediate advantage of his lack of attention and darted forward, grabbing the keys from his hand and running towards the Jaguar. She was inside the car, fumbling for the ignition, when he caught up with her. There followed a brief, undignified tussle which resulted in Jack Dawlish hauling Gina unceremoniously out of the car.

He held her easily, her feet dangling several inches from the ground and her back pressed uncomfortably close to his chest as he fought to retrieve his keys from her tightly clenched fist. Gina battled to be free, her breathing becoming ragged as tears of anger and humiliation pricked her eyes. One arm pinned her body close to his, as immovable as a band of steel, so she kicked out instead. Jack swore as one high-heeled shoe connected with his shin, but his hold only tightened.

'Stop fighting me,' he commanded. 'You can't win,' he added, his voice soft in her ear, his breath warm against her cheek, and Gina abruptly ceased her futile struggle. Her heart was beating wildly and she was suddenly aware of the proximity of his body, of his arm pressing against her breasts. She licked her suddenly dry lips, let him take back his keys, then pushed weakly at his restraining arm.

'Let me go,' she whispered.

'Did no one ever teach you to say "please" and "thank you"?' he murmured, but he released his hold, albeit reluctantly. Holding her soft, squirming body against his had afforded him more pleasure than he cared to acknowledge, even to himself. Desiring Gina Bruce was definitely not part of the plan! He was sure her father had not had this in mind when he had asked Jack if he thought he could handle the twins! Handle, yes, manhandle, no.

Gina gave a huge sigh of relief when his arm dropped away from her, and she moved forwards, then cried out in pain and clutched the back of her head.

'You're pulling my hair!'

'Of course I'm not, it's caught in my button. Hold still,' he said firmly, and Gina gritted her teeth, forced to stand and suffer his fingers in her hair, feeling his hands brushing the suddenly sensitised skin at the back of her neck.

'Hurry up!' She was unable to endure it any longer and tried to twist away.

'Stand still.' His hands rested briefly on her shoulders. 'You're making it worse.' After what seemed an age, the last silky strand was loose and Gina stepped away from him.

'You're free of me – for now. Enjoy your weekend,' he said with mock politeness. 'Make the most of it,' he advised, reminding her that she had only two more days of liberty before he took control of her life. Gina gave him a withering look that should have felled him to the ground, but didn't comment and waited with ill-concealed impatience while he moved the Jaguar.

As soon as there was sufficient space, she jumped into her own car and reversed down the drive, then backed out on to the main road with scant regard for any passing traffic. Half afraid he might yet pursue her, she drove off at speed, wanting to put as much distance between them as she could.

When she felt safe, she pulled over and tried Gavin's mobile phone but it was switched off, so she continued on her journey. She was damned if she would tamely submit to Jack Dawlish's tyranny, and her anger sustained her throughout the journey back to London as she sought desperately to find a way out of the situation she was in. No immediate solution sprang to mind, but she was sure she would think of something – she just had to!

'We might as well face it – I'm broke,' Gina declared glumly to her twin later that evening as she tossed her latest bank statement aside in disgust at its contents.

He had arrived an hour earlier, bearing a bottle of wine and a large pizza, for a 'council of war'. His visit followed a frantic phone call from Gina who, upon reaching the sanctuary of her home, had suddenly realised the enormity of Jack Dawlish's intentions. If he carried out his threat – and she had no doubt he had meant every cruel word he had flung at her – then the flat she loved would not be her home for very much longer.

'Look at the lease,' she waved it at Gavin. 'The tenant is Bruce Casuals – and that's Jack Dawlish now, isn't it?'

'Afraid so,' he agreed. 'I can help you out with cash. Both Emily and I work full time for the company – even Jack Dawlish can't refuse to pay our salaries.'

'I wouldn't count on it,' Gina warned him. 'Thanks for the offer, but no thanks,' she smiled at him, well aware of his huge mortgage repayments and overdrawn bank balance. 'I'll think of something,' she said brightly with rather more conviction than she actually felt. She fell silent and gnawed absently at her lower lip, her brow furrowed as she sought for inspiration.

'This whole situation is ridiculous!' she exclaimed. 'I own twenty per cent of Bruce Casuals and fifty per cent of "The Beeches", yet I haven't enough cash to pay the phone bill! Can I sell my shares? And the house?'

'We can sell the house, but with Dawlish as co-executor

– and squatter – he can probably delay that if he wants to,'
Gavin said glumly. 'As for your shares, well no one would
want a minority shareholding,' he dashed her hopes.

'Maybe Jack Dawlish would?' Gina suggested. 'He
doesn't really want me in the company, any more than Dad
did. You could sell yours too, and let him have the lot!
You could move to London and make a fresh start,' she
enthused, but Gavin shook his head.

'Even if I decided to leave the company, Emily
wouldn't want to move away from her parents and all her
friends in Falworth,' he said. 'Besides, why should
Dawlish want to buy us out when he already has control?'

'To get rid of us?'

'He's a sadist – he's going to enjoy cracking the whip,'
Gavin said flatly.

'Oh,' Gina sighed, then brightened. 'I can sell my car!
It's a liability in London, any how.'

'I guess so,' Gavin sounded doubtful. 'You wouldn't get
much more than five thousand pounds for it though.'

'So? That will last for a while. And I can go to the bank
– they might be prepared to tide me over until we can
sell the house,' she continued. 'And those Chelsea vases
– they're insured for ten thousand,' she nodded towards
a pair of matching eighteenth-century vases on the
windowsill. She had brought them from Falworth
when she had first moved to London. 'I suppose they're
really part of Dad's estate, but what Jack Dawlish doesn't
know won't hurt him – or me,' she laughed, feeling an
upsurge of optimism, a glimmer of hope. But Gavin
only scowled.

'You shouldn't have to sell your possessions to continue
living here! That Jack Dawlish has a real cheek. I know
for a fact that he's a director of half-a-dozen companies
and I bet he takes a fee from every one of them without

doing much more than attending the occasional board meeting.'

'He isn't taking any money out of Bruce Casuals though, is he?' Gina pointed out. Gavin gave a short, mirthless laugh.

'No, not so far. A shrewd move that. He knows it will be harder for us to contest the will if he isn't profiting from his inheritance,' he said bitterly.

'Is that why?' Gina felt irrationally disappointed.

'Of course – what other motive could he have? God, this whole thing stinks!' Gavin said savagely. 'I can't believe Dad wanted this to happen. He was happy to finance you living here – he didn't want you involved in running the company.'

'Tell that to Jack Dawlish,' Gina said heavily. 'He seems to know an awful lot about us,' she mused, still incensed by the existence of the dossier he had produced from his briefcase. 'Where did he get his information – from Dad?' The idea was extremely distasteful to her, but she couldn't imagine how else he had learned details of her past.

'I suppose so,' Gavin shrugged. 'Dawlish has stayed at the house a lot recently.'

'Do you think he knew what was in the will? He didn't look very surprised,' she remembered.

'He probably dictated the entire thing,' Gavin said moodily, reaching out to pour more wine. 'I should have brought two bottles,' he grimaced, showing her the empty bottle.

'Don't look at me – I've barely drunk any of it,' she protested, then scrambled to her feet. 'You'd better have some coffee,' she worried, thinking of his drive back to the coast.

'Don't bother,' Gavin followed her into the kitchen. 'Do

you fancy a couple of hours at a club? It would do us both good,' he encouraged. Gina hesitated, then shook her head.

'Not for me. I'm tired and I don't feel like getting changed and made up,' she said. ' But you go. When I phoned Sophie earlier to tell her I might not be able to help out any more, she mentioned she and the others were going to The Gemini Club tonight – why don't you join them? They'd love to see you.'

'I think I will,' Gavin decided, reaching for his jacket. 'Oh, I'd better ring Emily – I told her I wouldn't be late.'

'Go ahead.' Gina set about preparing coffee for herself while he phoned Emily, then walked with him to the door. 'Take a key in case you want to stay overnight,' she said, rummaging for her spare set and handing them to him. 'Thanks for coming over – I was in a bit of a panic earlier,' she admitted. 'I'm OK now though,' she added, and Gavin grinned.

'That's better. We won't let the creep grind us down, will we?' he asked softly. 'Goodnight, little sister.'

'Goodnight. And I'm twenty minutes older than you, little brother,' she called after him. He acknowledged her words with a brief wave, then walked off in the direction of the Kings Road, leaving his car in the parking space he had managed to find earlier.

Gina went back inside the flat and curled up in an armchair to drink her coffee. With Gavin's departure, some of her uncertainty over the future returned and she switched on the TV in an effort to banish her fears. She had always known financial security and it was more than a little frightening to have the comforting bulwark of wealth removed so abruptly.

'Why did you do it, Daddy?' she whispered forlornly. Why had he practically disinherited Gavin after all his hard work and determination to carry on the family business, which was all Peter Bruce had asked of him? Gavin had excelled at sport, representing his county in both cricket and rugby, and would have chosen to pursue a career in either one had it not been for their father's insistence that he must join the company and prepare to take it over in due course.

Why had a virtual stranger been given control, not only of the business, but also of the twins' lives? And why had their father chosen Jack Dawlish, of all people! She stirred uncomfortably as a vision of him rose, unbidden, in her mind. Try as she might, it was proving impossible to banish the memory of those strong arms around her as he had lifted her bodily from his car, clasping her to the hard length of his body. Never had she felt so helpless, so humiliated. And how he had revelled in her frailty!

With an exclamation of impatience, Gina jumped up and began restlessly pacing the room, determined not to allow Jack Dawlish to dominate her thoughts. Who cared what he thought of her and her lifestyle anyhow? Admittedly, she wasn't a career girl – so what? It was none of his business what she did with her life, she told herself as she switched off the TV and prepared for bed. It was just a great pity he seemed intent on making it his business.

The insistent ringing of her bedside phone jolted her awake and, never at her best first thing in the morning, she fumbled blearily for the receiver.

'Mm?'

'Gina. It's Jack Dawlish. I'd like to speak to Gavin.' The crisp, cool tone banished sleep and Gina sat up abruptly. Were they to have no respite from the wretched man? Besides, Gavin wasn't here – at least, she hadn't heard him return, she thought, struggling to force her reluctant brain into some semblance of working order.

'Gina!' His voice was sharp. 'Don't play games. I've just spoken to Emily and she told me he drove over last night to hold your hand. Just put him on,' he ordered tersely.

'All right!' she snapped back. 'You woke me up. Hold on and I'll go and get him.' She scrambled out of bed and hurried to the spare room.

It was empty. But the bed had been slept in she noticed at once, and she called his name, banging on the bathroom door in passing. There was no reply and she moved into the sitting room, pulling back the drapes to check if his car was still outside. It was, so he isn't on his way home, she thought, making her way slowly back into her bedroom and pausing before picking up the receiver.

'Hello? I'm sorry, but he isn't here,' she said, and the short silence which followed told her that Jack Dawlish didn't believe her.

'Is he on his way back to Falworth and his wife?' he asked, with a distinct edge to his voice and Gina stifled a sigh. Oh God, this was even worse! He evidently thought Gavin had spent the night with another girl!

'Er, no, his car's still here. I guess he's slipped out for a newspaper, or something,' she said quickly. 'Do you want him to phone you back?' She crossed her fingers as she asked the question, knowing instinctively what Gavin's reaction to such a request was likely to be.

'That's not necessary. Tell him to meet me at his house at eleven-thirty. And tell him not to keep me waiting.'

'What do you want him for? Isn't he entitled to a weekend in peace?' Gina asked tartly.

'As he didn't bother turning up at the factory yesterday afternoon for a scheduled meeting, no, he isn't,' Jack

Dawlish retorted swiftly. 'It's my weekend too, but there are some matters I need to discuss with your brother before Monday.'

'Oh.' Gina hadn't realised Gavin had played truant. 'He was upset yesterday,' she excused him. 'You can hardly blame him for avoiding the factory when he had just discovered it had been handed to you on a plate!'

'Just tell him to be back here by eleven-thirty,' he said curtly, then rang off. Gina checked the time as she replaced the receiver – it wasn't even eight o' clock yet, plenty of time for Gavin to make the journey – *if* he returned to the flat soon. Where on earth could he be? She was worried, for it was unlike him to be up and about early in the morning, especially after a late night. At least he *had* returned so he wasn't lying in a drunken stupor some-where, she consoled herself and, shrugging off her concern, went to make coffee.

After she had gulped down two cups of hot, strong coffee, she went to take a shower and had turned on the jet before it occurred to her that Gavin might possibly drive off without speaking to her, thinking she was still asleep. She would hate for him to arrive home unprepared for his meeting with Jack Dawlish, so she dashed outside in her dressing gown and left a note under the windscreen wiper, telling him not to go until he had seen her.

She had showered and dressed in jeans and a sweater, and was sitting over a third cup of coffee, when she heard Gavin let himself back into the flat. She jumped up and went to greet him, sniffing appreciatively at the bag of warm croissants he handed to her.

'Ooh, lovely, thanks. Come and have some coffee,' she offered, heading back to the kitchen. 'You were up early,' she commented.

'Mm, couldn't sleep,' Gavin said briefly and, indeed,

dark shadows beneath his eyes proclaimed a wakeful night, Gina noted anxiously. Damn Jack Dawlish! This was all his doing!

'What's this about?' Gavin waved her note in front of her. 'I thought I'd got a parking ticket when I first spotted it,' he grimaced.

'Oh, sorry. You might prefer that actually,' she said slowly. 'Jack Dawlish phoned a while ago – he wants to see you at your house at half-past eleven,' she told him, then winced at his succinct response. He made no other comment though, and instead regaled her with the 'who had done what and with whom' the night before as they breakfasted. He seemed in no hurry to leave, and Gina grew increasingly concerned. No good could come of Gavin's thwarting Jack Dawlish – for now, at least, he held all the cards. And Gavin would be even worse off than she was if he and Emily were sacked from the firm.

'Aren't you going to meet him?' she ventured at last. 'Maybe he wants to suggest some sort of compromise?'

'Did he sound as if he did?' Gavin's eyebrows rose in disbelief.

'Er, no,' Gina had to admit. Affability hadn't exactly hummed down the phone lines.

'I thought not,' he said moodily.

'He might start making Emily's life miserable if you keep him waiting,' she said next, and that did make an impression on him.

'Yeah, you could be right,' he got heavily to his feet and handed her back her spare keys. 'Thanks for the bed. I'll let you know what happens.'

'Shall I come with you?' Gina asked impulsively, hating to see him go, particularly when he looked so strained and unhappy. Surely their father couldn't have really wanted this?

Gavin hesitated, then shook his head and forced a smile.

'No. Thanks for offering, but I'd rather you stayed well away from him. This is my battle – I'll fight it alone.'

'Since when have we fought battles alone?' she asked. He smiled again and touched her hand.

'I know. But this is different…' he frowned, struggling to put his unease into words. 'There's something odd about all this, something niggling at the back of my mind and, until I've figured out what it is, I'd prefer you to stay out of his way.'

'OK,' Gina said after a moment but, after he had gone, she mulled over ways in which she could help her twin. If she returned to Falworth, temporarily of course, she could give Gavin moral support while apparently meekly submitting to Jack Dawlish's demand that she be at the factory on Monday morning. Not too meekly, though, since she guessed he would be suspicious of her capitulation and so she would have to tread very carefully…

One thing she was determined on, and that was to keep her flat. It was her home and Jack Dawlish wasn't taking it from her, she resolved fiercely. And so, after lunch, she fished out the relevant documents for her car, half afraid she would discover it was registered to the company but, no, it was in her own name.

Her spirits rose a little at this first piece of good luck and she spent the afternoon touring the second-hand car salesrooms and returned, by cab, with a cheque for just over five thousand pounds in her handbag. Her home was secure, well, for a few months at least, she amended, remembering the high rent and other bills for which she was now responsible. Perhaps she had taken it all for granted in the past, she found herself thinking guiltily, then pulled herself together. Good grief – she'd soon be agreeing with Jack Dawlish's opinion of her!

Early on Sunday evening, she was relaxing and listening to music when the buzz of the entry phone proclaimed the arrival of a visitor.

'Yes?'

'Jack Dawlish,' he announced curtly.

'Oh!' Gina was taken aback. She hadn't expected to have to face him so soon, believing he had remained in Falworth over the weekend. His meeting with Gavin had gone reasonably well – he would receive no profit sharing and had been told to cut down on his expenses, but his salary would remain the same.

Gina bit her lip, wondering what he wanted, and her hand was shaking slightly as she reluctantly released the lock on the outer door of the building. She still hadn't worked out her strategy but, much as she would like to, there was nothing to be gained by refusing him admittance. However, her whole being cried out against having him in her home.

'Flat Two,' she said coolly, then opened the door of her flat and stood on the threshold; whatever he had to say to her could be said on the doorstep! The indignity she had suffered at his hands at their previous meeting still rankled heavily and she wished she were wearing something more formal than her jeans and a T-shirt, with her long hair swept back into a casual pony-tail and no make-up.

It took an enormous effort of will to face him, but she did so, her chin jutting mulishly, hands belligerently on hips, her stance belying the quickening pace of her heart-beat as he came to a halt in front of her. Somewhat to her surprise, his attire was as casual as her own; faded denims hugged his lean hips and long legs, a white shirt, unbuttoned at the throat, emphasised his dark good looks. But nothing could add warmth and humour to those ice-cold grey eyes, she thought, striving to conceal the apprehension she felt at his unexpected presence.

'What do you want?' she demanded rudely. One dark eyebrow rose at her tone, but other than that he remained impassive.

'I thought you might need help with your cases,' he drawled. 'I assume you have started packing up here?'

'You assumed wrong!' Gina ground out.

'Now why aren't I surprised?' Jack mused, then before Gina realised his intention, he pushed her unceremoniously back into the flat and followed, closing the door behind him and leaning against it, as if barring her escape. Gina swallowed nervously and took several prudent steps backwards before answering him.

'I haven't started packing because I'm not leaving. This is my home and I'm keeping it. And don't start moaning about money again – I'm taking over the lease personally. I'll pay my own rent from now on,' she informed him loftily.

'How?' Jack asked bluntly.

'That's none of your business.' Gina stood her ground, although it took every ounce of courage she possessed. Jack Dawlish seemed even taller and broader than he had on Friday. He was altogether too aggressively male for her prettily feminine flat, and she fervently wished him gone.

'Like hell it isn't,' he growled. Without warning, he pounced, grabbing her arm and pulling her closer, his eyes boring into hers. 'Where have you suddenly acquired money? Or should I ask, from whom?' he went on softly. 'I might have guessed you would try to take the easy way out,' he said contemptuously, and Gina gasped in outrage as she realised the implication behind his words. The insufferable pig!

'Let go of my arm! I don't have to tell you anything!'

she said furiously, trying in vain to pull free of his loath-some touch.

'No?' His fingers were hard on the soft flesh above her elbow.

'No! What does it matter to you who gave it to me? My father might have given you control of the company, but you don't own me!' she hissed, still struggling within his grasp.

'Someone evidently does,' he shot back then, as if sick-ened by the touch of her, he thrust her away from him so forcefully that she almost fell, and only saved herself from sprawling ignominiously at his feet by grabbing a chair. She straightened and glared her hatred at him, her dark eyes flashing with defiance.

'You're wrong about me. Again,' she said bitterly.

'Prove it,' he said tersely.

'Why should I?' Gina challenged him but, under his steely-eyed gaze, found herself moving to pick up her handbag. She didn't understand why his unjustified contempt hurt but it did, so she took out the cheque and held it out to him.

'I've sold my car.'

'You've done what?' Jack took three long strides and studied the cheque before raising his head and looking at her. 'You're that determined to remain here?' he frowned. Gina hesitated – would he somehow use the knowledge against her?

'It's my home,' she said finally. 'Besides, a car is a headache in this part of London – people are always nicking the residents' parking spaces,' she added, dismissing the loss of her car as if it were of no account. 'Now I can pay my rent until Gavin and I sell "The Beeches".'

'Five thousand pounds won't last long,' he warned.

'That's my problem,' she shrugged. Jack stared at her, a frown marring his features.

'Are you getting married?' he asked abruptly, and it was Gina's turn to stare. Then she grinned.

'Thanks for the offer, but no thanks,' she said sweetly. Jack counted slowly to ten. And then again. God give him patience!

'If and when I get married, it will be to a grown-up!' he responded cuttingly. 'That was not a proposal, as you well know. But it was a serious question – have you managed to convince some poor fool you'll make him a good wife?'

'I've no intention of being anyone's wife,' Gina sniffed. 'Why on earth are we having this pointless conversation?'

'Because, if you intend to remain single, sooner or later you will run out of capital. Can't you see that selling your car, then the house, is only a short-term solution?' he asked exasperatedly. 'What will you do then?'

'Something will turn up,' she muttered, deeming it unwise to tell him she hoped Gavin would be back in charge of the company long before she had used up her supply of funds. 'Anyway, I won't just be using up capital – I do have a job,' she reminded him.

'There's a job for you in Falworth,' Jack said quietly, and Gina's heart gave a lurch. Sure there was – helping Gavin rid them of Jack Dawlish! She was afraid he might divine her thoughts and kept her eyes lowered, silently warning herself not to arouse his suspicions by seeming eager to return.

'Doing what?' she asked mutinously. 'You made it perfectly plain on Friday that you consider me a liability to the firm.'

'I also said I intend making sure you pull your weight in future. Even if it means you working in the sewing room,' he added. Gina looked up sharply at that, and he smiled thinly at the expression of horror on her face. 'Don't worry. I abandoned that idea, albeit with some regret. Unfortunately, it wouldn't help the company's image if a director works on the factory floor. Besides, they're fast and efficient workers – you'd hold up production,' he added nastily, and Gina had to fight an almost overwhelming urge to inflict physical injury on him. Only the knowledge that she would fare badly in any such encounter prevented her from indulging in the satisfaction of slapping his hateful, sneering face.

'So what do you have in mind?'

'Is there any point in asking if you have computer skills?' Jack sighed, obviously expecting a 'no'. Actually, Gina could surf the Net with the best of them and kept in regular contact with her friends from finishing school, now scattered throughout Europe, by email, using the computer which was in her spare bedroom. She glanced over to quickly check that the door was firmly closed, hiding the computer from Jack's view, then smiled at him. Given the chance, he'd put her to work in the office until she was eligible to draw her pension!

'I'm afraid not,' she said regretfully. He hadn't expected anything else, so didn't pursue it.

'Actually, I want you to act as my hostess at a succession of dinner parties. We need to reassure existing customers that we're still in business and attract new ones. I know you did that very capably for your father.'

'Did he say so?' Gina asked quickly.

'Yes,' he nodded, and noted how her eyes lit up with pleasure. 'A lot of business can be accomplished over a pleasant, relaxing meal. He told me you can charm the men without alienating their wives, which is a rare quality.'

'Oh! I enjoyed doing it. I never thought of it as work,' Gina said guilelessly. 'He never said...' she broke off uncertainly as a slow smile spread over Jack's face.

'Well, well,' he drawled softly. 'So you did crave your father's approval, after all,' he said, with an unmistakable air of triumph which Gina neither understood nor liked. It was as if he had discovered some new weapon to use against her.

'Not at all,' she denied swiftly. 'I knew there was no point in even trying. I made the unforgivable mistake of being a girl. He wanted a son and heir to carry on the name and the business but me, well, I was surplus to requirements,' she finished bitterly, her lips twisting with the memory of a thousand rebuffs she had suffered before realising her place, or rather her lack of one, in her father's life.

'Oh dear, you poor little rich girl,' Jack mocked her. 'The best schools, here and abroad, expensive holidays, a life of idle luxury – you really have been badly treated, haven't you?'

'You know nothing about it!' Gina snapped, regretting the words which had betrayed her vulnerability.

'No?' he queried meaningfully, and Gina stared at him, remembering the dossier he had in his possession. He held her gaze for a long moment and it was Gina who had to break the contact. There was something about his air of supreme self-confidence which undermined her own self-esteem. She didn't deny the expensive schooling or the luxuries she enjoyed which many others did not, but none of that compensated for the rest. She and Gavin had lost their mother, been left with a cold and heartless father who had sent them away to separate schools. How unhappy they had been! Jack Dawlish didn't know that or, if he did, he didn't care. Like their father... With an effort, she forced her thoughts back to the present and glared at him.

'Surely you have someone else who can act as your hostess?' she asked ungraciously.

'Yes, of course. I'm not talking about my other interests, just Bruce Casuals. There has been a growing lack of confidence in the company since your father retired and I can regain lost ground much quicker if I have his daughter at my side. And if you can persuade Gavin to stop fighting me every inch of the way and listen to reason, the recovery will be even faster. We need to show everyone, employees, existing and potential customers, that we're all working together,' he finished.

'You can't blame Gavin for feeling resentful,' Gina leaped to her brother's defence. Jack Dawlish must be crazy if he thought she would work with him against her twin! Jack sighed heavily, but made no further comment on Gavin's behaviour.

'I have something else for you to do,' he said instead.

'What?' Gina asked warily.

'Stop being so suspicious!' he growled. 'All I want to do is turn Bruce Casuals back into a profitable company. Is that so bad?'

'It's Gavin's inheritance, not yours,' Gina said stubbornly.

'It won't belong to anyone if I don't make some radical changes!' Jack said impatiently. 'Would you and Gavin prefer to have forty-five per cent of a flourishing concern, or one hundred per cent of a bankrupt one?'

'We wouldn't go bankrupt – Gavin knows what he's doing,' Gina declared loyally.

'He's good in his own field,' Jack acknowledged, 'which is sales and marketing. But he's no businessman. If he had overall control, the bank would call in its loans within six months,' he said, sounding so confident that Gina lapsed into silence, unable to argue – she hadn't even known the loans existed! And, she realised, the company must have been in financial difficulties for her father to have approached Jack Dawlish in the first place.

'What is it you want me to do?' she asked cautiously.

'The whole factory needs a face-lift. It's shabby and run-down, which hardly inspires confidence. Do you think you can organise that without bothering me with details?'

'Of course I can,' she said stiffly. In fact, she'd quite enjoy the task but she wasn't about to tell him that!

'Good. We'll discuss a budget tomorrow and you can make a start immediately.'

'Can we afford it? I thought we were almost bankrupt?' she reminded him caustically.

'We can't afford not to,' he told her, ignoring her sarcasm. 'I'm only talking about the parts customers see – the grounds, the outside of the buildings and the reception areas. So? Do we have a deal?' he asked. Gina lowered her eyes. It was better than she had hoped for. She would be in Falworth to help Gavin, but with Jack Dawlish thinking it was his idea and against her own wishes. However, she sensed he was watching too closely for her reply, as if she had somehow unwittingly aroused his suspicions.

'You've forgotten one thing,' she said casually.

'Oh?' he frowned. 'What might that be?'

'My salary. Or director's fee.' She faced him squarely. 'I don't care what you call it, so long as I'm paid for being in Falworth. If you don't agree to that, I'll stay here and get another job to supplement what I earn with Sophie,' she shrugged, as if indifferent to his response.

'Fair enough,' Jack nodded. 'If you pull your weight,

you'll be paid adequately. Deal?' he repeated softly and held out his hand. Gina wavered for a moment longer, suddenly beset by doubts and wondering if Gavin would be angry with her for not doing as he said and keeping well away from the enemy. And making deals with Jack Dawlish had to be on a par with forming a pact with the devil! Nevertheless, she put her hand in his.

'Deal,' she echoed. His grip was firm and business-like. There was no logical reason to pull away from him, but she did, uncomfortably aware of strange, tingling sensations engendered by the contact of his warm flesh against hers.

'Get your things together,' he said briskly. 'You can drive down with me now.'

'Oh, that's not necessary,' Gina said quickly. 'I'll come down in the morning…by train,' she added, belatedly remembering she no longer owned a car.

'I'd prefer it if you came now,' Jack said, quite pleasantly, but implacably. 'I have some papers to look through, so you can add chauffeuse to your other duties. You seemed anxious to get behind the wheel of my car on Friday,' he reminded her, with a glint of amusement in his eyes. Gina cringed inwardly at the memory of her humiliation at his hands, both literally and emotionally, and decided he was just as capable of forcing her into his car as he had been of dragging her out of it.

'Very well,' she conceded unwillingly, and moved to do his bidding.

chapter three

Any pleasure Gina might have derived from driving the
Jaguar was quickly dissipated as she realised Jack was
using the opportunity of being the passenger to study her
closely. He didn't even make a pretence of producing the
papers he had mentioned, but settled back comfortably in
his seat and went on to the attack while she was still
concentrating on mastering the controls of the powerful
car.

'Why was Gavin here on Friday night?' he rapped out,
before they had travelled more than a hundred yards.

'Why do you think? We were deciding how best to get
rid of you! I thought strychnine would be best but Gavin
says arsenic is more painful, so arsenic it is!' she snapped,
but he only laughed.

'You misunderstood the question. I have no doubt the
two of you felt you had things to discuss, but why here?
You were in Falworth...'

'...And couldn't wait to leave,' Gina interjected. Jack
inclined his head in acknowledgement.

'Even so, why was Gavin here overnight? I don't know
if you'll even care,' his voice hardened, 'but Emily looked
very unhappy yesterday morning when Gavin hadn't
arrived home.'

'I don't see why she should have,' Gina said, rather impatiently. 'She knew where he was. And he did phone her.'

'It was obvious to me that she hadn't expected him to
stay out all night,' Jack continued, disapproval evident
in his voice.

'He didn't intend to,' Gina protested. 'He brought some wine with him and we were talking, and just didn't realise how late it was, or how much he'd had to drink,' she explained, carefully omitting any mention of Gavin's decision to meet up with old friends at a nightclub, sensing that would meet with even more censure. 'It would have been irresponsible of him to have driven home,' she added virtuously. The man beside her snorted at that, as if unimpressed by Gavin's observance of the laws concerning drink driving.

'Why are you so concerned about Emily, anyhow?' Gina went on, remembering anew how her sister-in-law had been the only person he'd had a kind word for at the reading of the will. 'Are you trying to steal Gavin's wife as well as his inheritance?' she asked snidely, and immediately regretted her accusation. Jack became totally still, yet she sensed the barely-suppressed fury in him and licked her lips nervously, awaiting the retribution she was sure would follow her remark.

'Someone ought to teach you some manners, young lady,' he said softly, but with such deadly menace that Gina felt a cold finger of fear touch her spine. 'One more crack of that nature and you'll discover just how tough I can be,' he warned. Gina didn't doubt it for a moment, and she gripped the steering wheel tightly, aware that her palms were damp.

'You mean things can get even worse than they already are?' She tried to sound flippant, but heard the betraying tremor in her voice. She was sure Jack had heard it too.

'Oh yes,' he knew exactly what – or rather who – was her Achilles heel. 'Your behaviour will influence my attitude towards Gavin – and his future with the firm. He's an angry young man right now, with some justification,' he acknowledged fairly, 'and I'm prepared to make some allowances for his un-cooperation – to a certain point. But if you cross me, I'll make him wish he had never been born,' he asserted grimly. 'Do I make myself clear?'

'Perfectly,' Gina ground out, hating him as she had never thought she could hate any person. 'I…I'm sorry,' she managed, but couldn't resist adding, 'Emily wouldn't be interested in you anyhow. She loves Gavin.'

'You don't have anything to worry about then, do you?'

'No,' Gina said, but rather uncertainly, taking a sideways glance at the man beside her. He was too cold and harsh to be attractive to her, but there was no denying his good looks, she admitted grudgingly. He exuded a raw masculinity, yet made no effort to charm or utilise his sexuality. But of course that air of remoteness and self-sufficiency could pose a challenge to some women. But not Emily, she concluded, with relief. 'No, I don't,' she said more firmly and concentrated on her driving.

'I'm surprised you care about your brother's marriage,' Jack remarked, after a moment. Gina shot him a puzzled glance.

'What an odd thing to say. Of course I care.'

'About Gavin, yes, but Emily? I gained the distinct impression that you don't like her very much.'

'Really?' Gina refused to be drawn. In fact, she envied Emily her close, loving relationship with her parents, whom she still saw or telephoned every day, but wild horses wouldn't make her admit any such weakness to Jack Dawlish.

'Do you think she tricked Gavin into marrying her?' Jack persisted. Gina shrugged.

'I've never thought about it – it takes two to make a baby,' she said airily. Actually, she had wondered if Emily had deliberately become pregnant, but Gavin had seemed happy enough about the baby and subsequent hasty marriage, so she had kept her doubts to herself. And after the miscarriage, he had been genuinely upset and had never even hinted that he might want out of the marriage. Quite the reverse, in fact. She knew they were hoping for another baby.

'Something about her bugs you,' Jack persisted. Gina stifled a sigh. What was this? Twenty questions?

'If you must know, my father's attitude bugged me, as you call it. He never uttered one word about them being careless or immoral, but if I had come home and told him I was pregnant, well, he'd have gone ballistic! It would have been never-darken-my-doorstep-again-you-trollop...' She stopped speaking abruptly. Why on earth was she giving Jack Dawlish any information about herself, or her feelings, when she knew he would only use such knowledge against her?

'I see,' Jack smiled slightly. Peter Bruce had been afraid Gina resented her twin's closeness to another woman, when apparently it was her father's ready acceptance of a daughter-in-law that had hurt her. It was a pity he had never asked. In fact, it was a pity the older man had never talked to the twins about a whole range of subjects. 'Fathers are usually more Victorian in their attitude towards their daughter's sexuality than they are towards their son's,' he said lightly. 'Double standards, I know, but as old as Time.'

He said nothing more and Gina began to relax a little as she gained confidence, becoming accustomed to the car and enjoying the power beneath the bonnet. She gradually increased her speed as they left London behind and half-expected him to tell her to slow down, but he didn't. In fact, he seemed perfectly at ease, more so than any other man she'd had the misfortune to have as a passenger. In her experience, they either criticised and constantly

warned of traffic hazards she had already noted, or patro-
nisingly told her she was 'quite a good little driver'. Even
Gavin sat, tense and tight-lipped, breathing an audible
sigh of relief when they reached their destination
unscathed, despite the fact that she had passed her driving
test at the first attempt while he had failed twice.

It was only when they neared Falworth, that it occurred
to Gina that Jack was a guest at 'The Beeches'. She
couldn't possibly stay there too. And, when her father had
said Jack was to stay at the house, he hadn't expected her
to be back in Falworth, she reasoned, as she turned the car
towards the centre of town.

'Taking the scenic route?' Jack enquired blandly.

'Er, no, I assumed you'd booked into an hotel,' she said.
Surely she didn't have to spell it out! 'You can't stay at
the house, not now you're insisting I move back.'

'At the last count, there were seven bedrooms and a
live-in housekeeper,' he drawled with evident amusement,
and Gina felt her cheeks redden.

'I know, but...'

'But nothing. I need to be there while I sort out years
of paperwork stacked in your father's study. Mary is
expecting us both. I phoned her earlier,' he added casually. So, he had been confident she would agree to accompany him to Falworth, Gina noted. 'We're still heading in
the wrong direction,' he pointed out. Gina braked sharply,
more sharply than was necessary, then silently reversed
into a convenient driveway and, not knowing what else to
do, headed towards 'The Beeches'.

She climbed slowly from the car, reluctant as ever to
enter the house which hadn't felt like home since her
mother's death. However, she was careful to keep her
features impassive, aware of Jack's eagle eye on her.

Mary had evidently been listening for the car and

bustled out to greet them. Bright, welcoming light spilling out on to the driveway as she pulled open the front door.

'Come inside and eat,' she urged them both. 'You must be famished.'

Gina wasn't in the least bit hungry – her stomach still churning with nerves – but she smiled and said nothing. She followed Mary into the kitchen, which was warm and filled with an appetising aroma of chicken casserole and baked potatoes. She stooped to make a fuss of Jasper, who had ambled over from his basket by the Aga, then she turned to Jack.

'I expect you'd prefer to eat in the dining room?' she asked, hoping he would say 'yes' and give her a brief respite.

'In solitary splendour?' One dark eyebrow arched. 'I don't think so.'

'Suit yourself,' she shrugged, as if indifferent to where he chose to eat, and took her place at the large, scrubbed pine table. She picked desultorily at the food on the plate Mary put before her, glad of the older woman's presence and of Jasper's, who had jumped up onto the empty chair beside her.

The kitchen was – usually – a relaxing place to be, one of the nicest rooms in the house Gina had often thought. It was old-fashioned, but warm and comfortable – Mary had seen to that over the years. She had always been kind to the motherless twins, and Gina suddenly realised that there would no longer be a job for her at 'The Beeches' once the house was sold.

'Has Mr Williams told you about your legacy?' she asked.

'Oh yes. It was a lovely surprise and so generous of your father,' Mary beamed. 'I wasn't expecting anything like that in his will.' Nor were Gavin and I, Gina thought wryly and caught Jack's quizzical eye on her. Damn the wretched man! Was he a mind reader too? She glared at him before turning back to Mary.

'I'm glad you have a nest-egg,' she told her. 'I expect Gavin and I will sell the house eventually,' she hinted.

'I've already assured Mary that I'll be responsible for her wages until the estate is settled,' Jack put in. 'And, with her culinary skills, she can have a job with me any time she likes,' he added with a warm smile for the house-keeper.

'I doubt she'll ever be that desperate,' Gina muttered then, remembering what he had threatened regarding her own behaviour having a direct bearing on his attitude towards her twin, smiled brightly as if she had been joking.

'That's very kind, but my sister has already asked me to go and live with her – she's been dreadfully lonely since her husband died, so the arrangement will suit us both very well. I'll be fine, so don't worry about me, poppet,' Mary leaned over and hugged Gina. 'I'll just go and switch on your electric blanket, although the bed should be aired...' She left the room on her errand and a short silence descended.

'Poppet?' Jack queried incredulously, and Gina flushed.

'Well, she has known me since I was a kid,' she mumbled defensively.

'So she has,' he agreed thoughtfully. 'Aren't you going to eat that?' he pointed to her almost full plate.

'I'm not very hungry,' she shook her head, and took advantage of Mary's absence to put some chicken on a side plate for Jasper. 'Don't be impatient – you know I have to check it for bones,' she scolded him lightly. But, after one sniff, Jasper turned up his nose at the food and wandered back to his basket.

'Never mind the cat, I'm ravenous,' Jack declared and

without further ado, reached across and swapped his empty plate for hers, then tucked into his second helping with obvious enjoyment. Gina was secretly glad he had spared her from one of Mary's scoldings about her lack of appetite, but wasn't about to show any gratitude.

'You'll get fat,' she told him sourly, although she had to admit there were no signs of over-indulgence on his body. He looked sleek and fit, and moved with the easy grace of a man accustomed to exercise.

'Possibly,' he agreed, not sounding unduly concerned. 'I can't resist home-cooked meals when the opportunity arises, which isn't often enough for my liking,' he confided, and Gina felt surprised he had let slip even this tiny weakness. In fact, it was the only personal detail about him she had learned, she realised – with a sense of shock, since he had seemed to dominate her thoughts and her life since their first meeting.

'You should get married then,' she said lightly.

'You think so?' He looked up and held her gaze for a moment, while Gina was cursing herself for a fool. Why on earth had she said that? What poor girl deserved him for a husband? She felt herself tense beneath his cool scrutiny and tore her eyes away.

'Mm, you wouldn't be such a bully if you had a wife,' she managed.

'Really?' A slight smile tugged at his mouth. 'You think I need the softening touch of a good woman, do you?' He had spoken as casually as she, yet Gina found herself imagining touching him, not in the way he had meant, but physically running her hands over his skin, seeking out the hard muscles and sinews, discovering for herself if his black hair was soft and fine beneath her fingers…

'Or a bad one,' she forced a cool, impersonal smile, and an appreciative grin lit up his face, transforming his features completely and changing him, most disturbingly, from a cold, unapproachable man into something resembling an attractive human being. Attractive? Who was she kidding? Drop-dead gorgeous, more like.

'That sounds more tempting,' he approved. 'But I think I'll settle for my mother's home-cooking.'

'Where is home?' Gina asked curiously.

'I was brought up on a farm – it's on the outskirts of a small village in the Wye valley,' he told her.

'Oh.' Gina was struggling to imagine him as a farmer's son. Jack misinterpreted her slight confusion.

'Near Wales,' he elaborated, sighing at her ignorance.

'I know that!' Gina said huffily, although she hoped he wouldn't ask her to pinpoint it on a map! Geography had never been one of her strongest subjects. 'Do your parents still live there?' she asked.

'My father lives abroad now, but my mother still lives on the farm – she inherited it from my grandfather. After the divorce, she rented out the land and turned the farmhouse into a Bed and Breakfast. She enjoys the company.'

'How often do you go back?' she asked next, and he grimaced.

'Not as often as I should. I don't have the time.'

'You'd have more spare time if you handed your shares over to Gavin,' Gina said promptly, and immediately a frown replaced the smile.

'I can't do that,' he said shortly.

'You mean, you won't,' Gina amended bitterly, and he inclined his head in acknowledgement. Why did I even bother? Gina thought crossly, as she stood up and began clearing the table, banging crockery with unnecessary force. The slight truce was obviously over, almost before it had begun, and the atmosphere in the room was now positively glacial.

'I'm going to bed,' she said abruptly.

'We'll be leaving for the factory at eight-thirty,' Jack said by way of reply, and she nodded silently. As she trailed tiredly upstairs, she wondered miserably what new battles would have to be fought the following day.

Gina tossed and turned a while, unused to the lack of traffic noise and fearful of what the future held for her and her twin, but eventually fell into a troubled sleep and awoke to the sound of the alarm clock. She stretched out her arm to silence it and turned sleepily back into the warmth of the bedclothes, before she remembered why she had set the alarm at such an ungodly hour. She sighed, then reluctantly pushed back the covers and clambered out of bed.

Yawning hugely, she thrust her feet into slippers and headed for the shower. 'The Beeches' had been built long before *en suite* facilities were the norm, and her bathroom was situated across the landing. As she opened her bedroom door, she walked straight into the solid wall of Jack Dawlish. Sleep vanished abruptly when she realised her palms were flat against the warmth of his chest, and that he had instinctively put out his arms to steady her. And was still holding her.

'Oh! I thought...' she pointed vaguely towards the other wing of the house, where her father's suite of rooms was situated, and also the guest rooms, one of which she had assumed Jack would be using.

'Good morning,' he smiled down at her, his gaze lingering on her slumberous eyes, sleep-flushed cheeks and tumbled hair.

'I...Good morning,' Gina stammered, acutely aware of the inadequacy of her cream lace nightdress. One shoestring strap had slipped down her arm, revealing rather too much of her breasts, yet she stood, immobile, as Jack slowly reached out and pushed it back up on to her shoulder. The gesture was somehow more erotic than if he had removed the strap instead of replacing it, and a great heat suffused her entire body. Gina felt incapable of movement and it seemed as if Jack had no intention of moving either. His hand remained on her shoulder, warm and still, until he began to gently caress the smooth skin beneath his fingers.

'How do you manage to look so desirable first thing in the morning when most women look like hell?' he murmured and Gina swallowed nervously.

'I don't know,' she whispered foolishly, waiting with bated breath for…for what exactly? She was devoid of coherent thought, conscious only of his touch, and his breath warm on her cheek. She gazed imploringly into his eyes, noticing the sweep of luxuriant, almost feminine, thick black lashes. He had to stop this, for it was somehow beyond her to break free, despite a warning from the sensible part of her brain which was screaming at her to move before it was too late.

Jack's hand moved slowly to the back of her neck, his fingers tangling into the silken strands of her hair, while his thumb sought out the frantic beating of the pulse at the base of her throat.

'Jack…' she pleaded huskily, although she couldn't have said whether she wanted him to release her or continue caressing her, and he looked at her mouth. She felt him shudder – or was it her? – then he bent his head and kissed her. For Gina, it was as if everything happened in slow motion. It seemed as if an age of yearning passed before his lips touched hers, before his hands slid to her waist, then to the small of her back, as he urged her pliant body against his.

He smelt of soap and toothpaste, cool, clean and very male, and she knew she shouldn't be allowing him to kiss her. Knew it, but still her arms crept up around his neck. Still she opened her mouth to him and moaned deep in her throat when his tongue began a gentle probing. She knew she must pull away, but couldn't bear to inflict such deprivation on herself.

Jack's hands at her waist seared her skin, and the thin nightdress offered him little hindrance when he began a deliciously slow exploration of her curves, holding her even closer and letting her feel the desire in him. Knowledge of his arousal should have shocked her into pulling free, but instead she felt a totally new ache begin deep within her and she sighed with pleasure as his hands moved slowly, tantalisingly, to cup her breasts in their thin veiling of lace. His thumbs caressed the jutting peaks of her nipples, causing her to whimper with the need for more, then he pushed aside the flimsy material and stood back a little to gaze his fill of her nakedness.

'You're beautiful, Gina, so beautiful,' he murmured, then lowered his head to her breasts, his tongue hot and wet against her sensitised flesh. She cried out and clutched his shoulders, needing to hold on to him for support. Wanting to hold on to him too, she realised dimly, running her hands over the broad expanse of his back, feeling the hard-packed muscles contract at her touch.

'Gina?' he asked thickly, his eyes – how could she have ever thought them cold, soulless? – hot with desire, a hectic flush staining his cheekbones. She nodded, acquiescing to the unspoken request, her body trembling with anticipation. He bent and picked her up, then paused by her open bedroom door to kiss her once more. Gina wrapped her arms around his neck and fervently kissed him back, dizzy with the new sensations she was experiencing. The books were right, she thought dazedly, the earth did move, and bells did ring…and ring.

'Hell!' Jack swore softly, then dropped her gently to her feet, and ran his hands distractedly through his hair. He knew he should be grateful for the interruption, but he had never felt less gratitude in his entire life. Whoever was on the other end of the telephone was in big trouble!

'What?' Gina swayed without his support.

'The phone,' he told her. 'Can't you hear it?' Gina could, but was quite happy to ignore it. Then the sound stopped and she smiled tremulously at him, but obviously for him the spell had been broken.

'Mary will be up here in a second,' he said tersely and, sure enough, Gina heard the housekeeper's tread on the stairs.

'Mr Dawlish? Telephone for you,' she called.

'I'll be right down,' he called back, without taking his eyes from Gina. His gaze was rueful, yet he turned and walked away from her without a word or a backwards glance.

Gina watched him go, filled with confusion and some resentment, then she clutched her nightdress to her and returned to her bedroom. Much too late, she snatched up her dressing gown and shrugged it on, belting it tightly at her waist. Saved by the bell, she thought mirthlessly, but saved from what? A bad mistake or the most wonderful experience of her life? A mistake, of course, she told herself firmly, becoming angry at her own behaviour. Any normal girl, with an ounce of common sense, would have moved past him and into the bathroom, or retreated back into the privacy of her bedroom. But not Gina Bruce! Oh no, she had to stand there, mesmerised, offering herself so wantonly it was hardly surprising he had reacted as he had!

You're a fool! she berated herself. Of all the men to be seduced by, you have to choose him! A man who feels nothing but contempt for you; a man who has taken Gavin's inheritance. Suddenly, she felt swamped with guilt and self-loathing. Her first loyalty was to her twin. If they couldn't rely on each other... Had Jack been following her father's advice and trying his favourite – albeit usually futile – method of 'divide and conquer' in his dealings with the twins? She felt sick at the very thought and shuddered at the enormity of what she had almost done, leaning against the wall until it occurred to her that Jack might come back upstairs when he had finished his phone call, expecting to continue what they had started!

That thought galvanised her into action and she slowly eased open the door and peered cautiously out into the hallway, before running the short distance to the bathroom and locking herself in. She turned on the shower and stood beneath the hot spray, rubbing briskly at her body to try and erase the memory of his touch.

She had to summon up all her courage to go downstairs, dithering in her room until she lost patience with herself and deliberately cultivated anger as a defence against the storm of bewildering emotions he had stirred within her. Honestly! Skulking around her own home, bolting her door as if she were the intruder, not him!

She squared her shoulders and stalked down the stairs to discover that he was on the phone. Still! With no thought for her, or the situation he had left behind! She glared balefully at him as she passed, but he was too engrossed in his conversation to notice, which only fuelled her irritation.

Actually, Jack was acutely aware of her but was determined to behave as if the kiss had meant nothing to him. He cursed himself as a fool for giving way to his base instincts – what on earth had possessed him? He needed to retain the upper hand over both Gavin and Gina, and his task at Bruce Casuals would be a hundred times more difficult than it was already if Gina believed he was falling for her undoubted charms. Fortunately, she had unwittingly given him a way out – her suspicions regarding his intentions towards Emily, completely groundless though they were, would serve his purpose most effectively.

Gina went into the kitchen and poured herself a cup of coffee, refused Mary's offer of a cooked breakfast, and was studiously reading the newspaper when he finally put in an appearance. She pretended not to have noticed him and waited for him to speak.

'Ready to go?' he asked casually, as if nothing had happened. Gina had been dreading a scene, or a leering comment, but his easy dismissal of what had transpired earlier infuriated her more than anything else could have done. However, she carefully schooled her features, glanced up at him and tossed the newspaper aside.

'Yes, I'm ready,' she said coolly and stood up, smoothing her narrow skirt over her hips. 'And yes, I do accept your gracious apology,' she smiled, saccharine-sweet, and moved past him to study her appearance in the hall mirror, leaning forward to ostensibly check her lip gloss while watching his reflection.

'You want an apology?' Jack looked and sounded amused! 'If you walk around half-naked and throw yourself into my arms, you can expect a healthy male reaction,' he informed her, as if the whole incident had been at her instigation!

'This is my home!' Furious, Gina swung round to face him. 'I assumed I had that part of the house to myself, as usual, and I certainly did not expect to be assaulted!' She drew herself up to her full height but, even in high heels, she was still forced to look up at him.

'Assaulted?' Jack repeated, no longer amused, but she felt he still wasn't taking her complaint seriously. 'Strange, but I'm sure I didn't hear you scream for help,' he said caustically. 'Or even ask me to stop,' he added, raising one dark eyebrow. Gina flushed hotly.

'No, well, I was half-asleep and…'

'Aroused?' he suggested, his smile back in place.

'No!' she denied crossly.

'Yes, you were,' he contradicted. 'There's no reason to get worked up about it, Gina,' his voice softened a little. 'After all, nothing happened,' he added. Gina stared at him incredulously. Nothing happened? But to insist otherwise would only alert him to the effect his love-making had had on her, she realised, and summoned up a cool smile.

'As you say,' she agreed lightly. 'But you are no gentleman,' she couldn't resist adding. Jack burst out laughing.

'And you are no Victorian Miss who needs smelling salts every time she's kissed by a man,' he retorted, then checked his watch. 'Come along – or you can walk,' he told her. Gina poked out her tongue at his retreating back, but followed him out to the car.

It was a silent, but mercifully swift, journey to the factory but, as the car swept through the entrance, Gina couldn't resist asking if, as part of the refurbishment, she should have the sign above the large iron gates amended to read 'Dawlish Casuals'.

'Don't be childish!' Jack snapped, as he braked to a halt in the space which had previously been reserved for her father.

'I take it that was a "no"?' Gina pushed her luck as she clambered from the car. Jack nodded curtly, bestowing upon her a glance of extreme irritation.

'Arrange for the painters to do the exterior first, then reception,' he began issuing orders as he walked towards the office block, evidently taking it for granted that she would follow in his wake and obey every dictum.

'I thought you were going to leave it to me? That you didn't want to be bothered with details?' she reminded him crossly, almost having to run to keep up with his long strides.

'Very well. But I want to see the estimates for the work before you give the go-ahead,' he warned.

'Of course.' Gina was happy to comply with that, since she had no doubt he was capable of making her personally responsible for any bills he considered to be excessive.

She turned at the sound of furious car-horn tooting from behind her, and smiled broadly at Gavin. He, however, did not return her smile. In fact, he seemed less than thrilled to see her. Jack had also turned and paused then continued on his way. This was too public a place for a confrontation with an angry young man.

'Hi,' Gina greeted her twin.

'What on earth are you doing here?' Gavin scowled at her.

'Helping you, of course,' Gina told him. 'I know you wanted me to stay in London, but this concerns me too.'

'Haven't I got enough problems right now without worrying about you staying at "The Beeches" with him? I take it he is still there?'

'Um, yes,' Gina couldn't quite meet his gaze. 'But so's Mary,' she pointed out. 'And he's paying her wages which I can't afford to do. Can you?'

'No,' he admitted. 'I still don't like it. I don't understand why he's even interested in Bruce Casuals – it's small fry compared to the other companies he's involved with that all have multi-million pound turnovers. By the way, I spoke to James Cameron yesterday…'

'On a Sunday?' Gina raised an eyebrow. Their father's accountant was usually on a golf course every weekend. He claimed it was the only way to stay out of the divorce court.

'Yes, I cornered him in the clubhouse. I felt sure Dad couldn't just hand over control to Dawlish, but apparently he could. It dates back to when Grandfather Bruce set up the company. The Articles of Association don't allow you or me to veto…'

'Don't blind me with science,' Gina interrupted again. 'You're telling me our seats on the board never entitled us to argue with Dad?' Why were they surprised? she thought. And, to be honest, had they really cared so long as the dividend cheques arrived promptly? She certainly hadn't. It was unfair on Gavin though.

'Basically, yes,' he sighed then said, 'I'd love to see that letter David Williams handed to Dawlish,' he mused, a slow smile spreading over his face as he looked meaningfully at Gina.

'What? Oh no,' she said quickly wishing, for once, that she couldn't read his mind. 'I am *not* searching his room for that letter,' she informed him, and hoped he mistook her reddening cheeks for signs of anger, not confusion at the prospect of being in Jack's bed. Er, no, not *bed*. Bedroom. Bed*room*.

'He's probably left it in Dad's study. Or his briefcase,' Gavin said.

'I thought you wanted me to stay away from him?' she reminded him nervously.

'And you said you wanted to help,' Gavin rejoined swiftly. 'I'm telling you, Gina, there's something weird about all this. He's not in it for the money, so he must have a personal reason. I need to know what it is,' he added, sounding so frustrated that Gina wavered.

'If I get an opportunity, I'll try and find it,' she capitulated, even while cringing at the very thought of snooping through Jack's private papers. Even worse, being caught snooping…

'Only if you're sure he's well out of the way,' Gavin cautioned. 'Don't take any risks. I'll be back late tomorrow.'

'Back? From where?' Gina panicked a little.

'I'm going to Birmingham. I only stopped by to check the mail,' he told her.

'Oh, great,' Gina muttered. She was beginning to wish she had stayed in London. And, if Jack discovered she was spying on him, she would no doubt wish she had never been born…

chapter four

Gina followed Gavin into the reception area, where Emily was already ensconced behind her desk. Teacher's pet, Gina thought uncharitably, still annoyed by Jack's championing of Gavin's wife, and his insinuations that Gavin neglected her.

'Hello,' Gina nodded coolly, and received an even curter nod from her sister-in-law in return. Emily was definitely not pleased to see her. Tough! Gina shrugged and continued on her way up the stairs that led to the suite of management offices. Miss Pettit, who had been Peter Bruce's secretary for as long as Gina could remember, greeted her with a warm smile.

'Hi, I'm glad someone's got a smile for me,' Gina perched on her desk and leaned over to open the top drawer. 'No toffees, Petty?' she asked in mock dismay, for it had been some years since Petty had ceased her habit of providing illicit sweets for the twins.

'My PA will be faxing some papers through shortly,' Jack appeared briefly in the doorway of Peter Bruce's office. 'Let me have them as soon as she does, will you?'

'Certainly,' Petty said, then she looked enquiringly at Gina once the door had closed again behind its new occupant. 'What's going to happen, Gina?' she asked worriedly. 'There's all sorts of rumours going around. Is Mr Dawlish staying on permanently?'

'Not if Gavin can help it,' Gina said promptly, then clapped her hand over her mouth. 'Oh, forget I said that please,' she begged. 'I think he'll be around for a while,' she paused, not sure how much to divulge. But Petty had been here forever, and Gina was certain her father had trusted her absolutely. 'I don't know if Dad said anything to you, but he changed his will to leave Jack Dawlish in charge.'

'Oh, poor Gavin! No, I didn't know about that,' she said, then her gaze went to the closed office door. 'I've always worked for your father, as you know. Do you think Mr Dawlish will want me to stay on? I know he has his own secretarial staff – I don't want some bimbo coming here from London and ruling the roost.' Her brow was creased with worry and Gina was quick to reassure her.

'I'm sure he'll want you to stay,' she said and hoped her confidence wasn't misplaced. 'This place would fall apart without you here. You know what a muddle it is when you're on holiday for a couple of weeks!'

'True,' Petty smiled. 'And I'll have the money your father left me. I can always leave and get a part-time job in the town if I don't like the changes around here,' she added darkly, then put aside her own worries to ask what Gina was doing at the factory.

'Oh, watching Gavin's back actually,' Gina grinned, 'but Jack Dawlish thinks I'm here to organise some redecorating! What colour scheme would you like up here?' she asked. They chatted for a few minutes further until Jack reappeared, asked Gina if she hadn't got any work to do, and summoned Petty, rather peremptorily, into the office. Gina mouthed 'Good luck', then took herself off to Gavin's empty office to make some preliminary phone calls regarding the task she had been assigned.

When she had successfully cajoled a local firm into coming out that afternoon to provide estimates, she took paper and pen and wandered around the buildings, deciding on what needed to be done. Wherever she went, from the sewing room to the canteen, to packing and despatch and to the offices, she encountered the same concern for the future that Petty had expressed, and she experienced a mounting feeling of inadequacy in the face of such anxious questioning. It was daunting to have grown men and women looking to her for answers and reassurance that their jobs were secure. To realise that, now her father was dead, she and Gavin – and Jack Dawlish, unfortunately – had to take on the awesome responsibility for the employees' livelihoods. When she had been forced to say, 'I'm sorry, I don't know,' for the umpteenth time, she retraced her steps and went back upstairs.

'Petty? How many people work here?' she queried, ashamed she needed to ask.

'About three-hundred-and-fifty,' Petty said promptly. 'Why?'

'I just wondered,' she smiled vaguely. 'How did you get on with him?' she jerked her head towards her father's – now, seemingly, Jack Dawlish's – closed office door.

'I'm reserving judgement until I see how things work out,' Petty said cautiously. 'I have to say, he was perfectly pleasant to me,' she added fairly. 'I just feel so sorry for Gavin.'

'Me too,' Gina agreed, then she walked over to his office, knocked briefly, but entered without waiting for a reply. She figured that was courteous without being subservient.

Jack was on the phone but he beckoned to her to sit down, so she took a seat and waited while he finished his call. He had discarded his jacket and rolled back his shirt-sleeves, revealing strong, tanned forearms with a sprinkling of dark hair. Long fingers tapped an impatient tattoo on the desk as he listened, and Gina found her eyes drawn to the movement. Simply looking at his hands reminded her of their touch on her body, and a glance at his face set her pulses leaping at the memory of his mouth on hers, on her breasts…

With an effort, she tore her gaze away and moved to stand by the window with her back to the room. How she wished the morning's encounter had not occurred! Until he had touched her, she hadn't realised she had such a sensual side to her nature. She'd had plenty of boyfriends, had enjoyed their kisses and caresses, but it had never been difficult to call a halt. Nothing in the past had prepared her for her wanton response to Jack Dawlish – and she didn't even like the man! It was terribly confusing, to say the least.

'Did you come in here to enjoy the view, or do you want to talk to me?' Jack asked. He was pretty sure she hadn't told Gavin what had transpired outside her bedroom – and thank God, or rather the telephone, that it had never moved to *in*side her bedroom – for her brother had gone off to Birmingham without first trying to remove Jack's head from his shoulders! Could he hope to succeed where Peter Bruce had failed, by divide and rule? Their father had said they never kept secrets from each other, he remembered, and wondered why she had not told Gavin she had been 'assaulted' by a man he already hated, and would have been pleased to discover yet another reason for his dislike.

Gina visibly jumped at the sound of his voice. She had been too deep in thought to notice he had finished his phone conversation. He had swivelled round in his leather chair and was facing her, waiting for her to speak. For a moment she stared at him blankly, unable to recall what she had wanted to say to him.

'Well?' Jack prompted.

'Er, everyone's worried about their job,' she said finally. 'They're all asking me what's going to happen, and I don't know what to say to put their minds at rest.'

'I see,' he said quietly. 'I suppose there were bound to be rumours.' He paused then said, 'Ask Miss Pettit to put up a memo in the canteen for all the staff to read, will you? Let everyone know I'll be there at five-thirty to answer any questions.'

'Oh, thank you.' Gina was relieved to have some definite news to impart. 'And Petty? Is her job secure? She knows everything there is to know about the business – Dad often said he would be lost without her,' she told him earnestly. Jack smiled slightly, glad to discover that she didn't only care about herself and her twin.

'I definitely want her to stay on,' he assured her gravely.

'And you're not going to bring in one of your…' Gina just managed to bite back Petty's derogatory 'bimbo' and substituted, '…assistants?'

'No, they have enough to do in London while I'm down here. Miss Pettit can continue ruling the roost,' he said blandly. Too blandly? Gina looked at him sharply as he repeated Petty's earlier words, but there was nothing in his expression to indicate that he had overhead their conversation. 'Is that all you wanted?' Jack reached for the phone, evidently eager to be rid of her so he could make another call. Gina nodded and headed for the door, only to stop dead in her tracks when he began speaking.

'Emily? Jack Dawlish,' he said pleasantly. 'I wondered if you were free to join me for lunch today?' he continued. If Gina had been facing him, she would have known he was watching her, far more interested in her response than in Emily's. He smiled with satisfaction when Gina dropped to one knee to fiddle – unnecessarily he was sure – with the ankle strap on her shoe. He was determined she shouldn't gain the impression he was attracted to her. She had already accused him of being interested in Gavin's wife. Well, let her continue to wonder. In fact, let her believe he made a pass at every pretty girl who crossed his path, he thought, but was uneasily aware that the notion afforded him little pleasure.

'Good. Ten minutes? We'll take my car,' he said and hung up. 'Still here, Gina?' he asked, in mock surprise.

'Yes!' She swung round. 'What on earth are...' she began furiously.

'Think very, very carefully before you say something you'll regret,' Jack warned her grimly. Gina held her tongue, but with difficulty. What possible reason could he have for seeking Emily's company if he weren't attracted to her? She watched him as he silently sorted papers, littering the desk top, then got to his feet, reached for his jacket and shrugged it on, all as if he were oblivious to her presence.

'Is it something to do with Dad's will?' she asked finally, unwittingly hitting on the correct answer. Jack kept his face impassive. At least, he hoped he did.

'Why should it be?' he asked unhelpfully. Gina ground her teeth in annoyance.

'Well, she is a beneficiary and you're one of the executors,' she said, making a valiant effort to keep her temper in check.

'I meant to ask you about that,' Jack suddenly recalled her and Gavin's reaction to the legacy. 'Why did you and Gavin find it so amusing that Emily inherited the jewellery? Have the two of you already pawned it? Or exchanged the stones for paste?' He sounded deadly serious and Gina almost laughed.

'No, nothing like that. I wish it had occurred to me though!'

'What was so funny then?' he frowned, obviously annoyed by her levity.

'Oh, nothing much – just a private joke,' Gina said airily. Two could play at stonewalling!

'One which excluded Emily? Rather unkind of you, wasn't it?' Jack said coldly.

'Oh, for God's sake!' His championing of her sister-in-law made Gina see red. 'She only had to ask Gavin if she wanted to know that badly! It was nothing important.'

'So tell me,' he invited.

'No.' She knew she was behaving childishly, but was too irritated to care what he thought. Let him believe she and Gavin had concocted some Machiavellian plot to deprive Emily of her inheritance, if he so chose! He already thought the worst of them anyway, so one more bad mark against their characters couldn't make any difference to his attitude.

'Very well.' He gave her one final, cold glance before striding to the door. 'Enjoy your lunch – I believe the food in the canteen is adequate, if not exactly what you're accustomed to,' he added by way of a parting shot.

Gina grimaced at the closed door, then turned and watched from the window until he emerged from the building with Emily, and helped her into the passenger seat of the Jaguar. As he moved round to the driver's side, he paused and glanced up at the window, as if aware of her eyes on him. Gina dodged quickly out of sight, but wasn't fast enough to miss the mocking salute he gave before climbing into the car and driving away.

She groped blindly at the back of a chair and sat down heavily, trembling with the force of her emotions. What was he playing at? He had been furious when she had accused him of trying to steal Gavin's wife – had that been righteous indignation at the slur on his character, or anger at her spot-on perception?

And, even if there was an innocent explanation for his invitation, didn't he realise how quickly rumours were started and spread in a small town like Falworth? If he didn't, Emily certainly did, for she had lived here all her life and must know that being seen out with another man, even for lunch, would cause comment and raised eyebrows, especially while Gavin was away.

Her anger turned fully on her sister-in-law. Knowing how Gavin felt about Jack Dawlish, how could she be so disloyal as to offer him friendship? And it had better be nothing more than friendship, Gina thought grimly, filled with murderous rage at the very idea of Emily hurting her twin. She remembered what Jack had said concerning Emily's supposed unhappiness because Gavin had stayed in London overnight and wondered if he were encouraging her to exact some sort of revenge, perhaps hinting that Gavin was being unfaithful...

'Are you coming for some lunch?' Petty popped her head round the door to ask.

'What? Oh, yes, all right.' Seeing Petty reminded her of Jack's decision to speak to the workforce and she waited while Petty typed out a memo which they pinned to the notice board when they went to eat. Gina could have typed it herself, of course, but figured the fewer people who knew she could use a computer, the better.

Gina was outside talking to the decorator when Jack and Emily returned. She turned her back and pretended not to notice Emily's cheery wave, knowing she was still too angry and suspicious to act in a friendly manner, and afraid she might be provoked into a public argument. Jack came over to be introduced to Mr Jackson and Gina found herself scanning his shirt collar and then his mouth for any telltale traces of lipstick – almost like a jealous wife, she told herself disgustedly, and forced herself to look away.

She noticed, with mounting resentment, how he took charge of the discussion, and how the other man deferred to him, querying details on which Gina had already given her decision. She yawned, loudly and ostentatiously, and Jack turned on her with a look of stern rebuke, but his lips twitched slightly in amusement and Gina found herself reluctantly grinning back.

'Minx,' he growled with mock severity as Mr Jackson moved away to check the condition of the wooden window frames.

'I only yawned,' Gina protested her innocence.

'Hm. From boredom? Or are you exhausted after doing half-a-day's work?' he asked dryly.

'I have worked before!' she snapped, annoyed by his constant and largely unjustified criticisms of her lifestyle.

'You must tell me about it sometime…' he began.

'After all, it won't take long,' she finished for him, and he laughed out loud.

'I wasn't actually going to say that,' he assured her.

'Huh!' Gina wasn't convinced.

'Gina, about this morning,' he went on in a low voice. 'You were right – an apology was called for,' he said, and she felt her jaw drop. 'If you would prefer me to move to a hotel, just say so. I've no wish to make you feel uncomfortable in your own home.'

She stared at him, perplexed by his sudden change of heart. Only hours ago, he had blamed her for what had happened! Now he was apologising and offering to rid her of his unwanted presence. Why? she wondered suspiciously, and it took only seconds for her to realise why he was prepared to leave 'The Beeches'. Emily! With Gavin away so much, and Jack ensconced in the anonymity of a hotel…

'That won't be necessary,' she said, forcing her lips into a grimace of a smile. The rat! She wanted him where she could see him! 'I'm sure there won't be a recurrence of what happened this morning. And Dad did stipulate that you were to stay at the house,' she added virtuously.

'So he did.' Jack was watching her closely, his eyes narrowed at her no doubt unexpected reaction to his offer. Gina gazed back guilessly and fervently hoped he wasn't flattered by her apparent willingness to share the house. He probably was though. He was certainly arrogant enough to believe that she wanted a repeat performance! Still, anything was better than his pursuit of Emily, who was rather naïve and had, thus far, seen only a pleasant side to Jack's nature. She, Gina, had witnessed the hard, cold man who was the real Jack Dawlish, and was therefore immune to his seduction technique. Oh yeah? You weren't displaying much immunity this morning! whispered a devil on her shoulder. 'And, of course, you've always been such a dutiful daughter, haven't you?' Jack asked snidely. Gina's smile didn't falter, and he frowned a little as she failed to rise to his bait, but he let it pass. 'Very well, we'll leave things as they are for now. It's certainly more convenient for me to work at the house.'

'Good. That's settled then,' she said cheerfully.

'Hm.' He was still regarding her thoughtfully, then abruptly changed the subject. 'Come up to the office at five-thirty – we'll meet the workforce together and present a united front.'

'Certainly,' Gina agreed placidly. 'Five-thirty,' she repeated, and turned away from him.

The canteen was filled to capacity, but the hubbub of conversation quickly died down to a low murmur and all heads turned towards them when they entered. Rather self-consciously, her eyes lowered, Gina followed Jack as he walked the length of the room. Someone stood up and offered her a chair, which she accepted with a brief smile of thanks. She found herself sitting directly in front of Emily and turned to speak to her.

'How was lunch?' she asked casually. 'Go anywhere nice?'

'We only had a sandwich at the pub – we were at the bank for most of the time looking at your grandmother's jewellery,' Emily told her. 'I'm not sure if I'll ever want to wear any of it,' she went on dubiously. 'There's a rather nice cameo brooch though, but I certainly don't want to wear it if it reminds Gavin of his grandmother! She was a bit of a tyrant, wasn't she?'

'She was, yes,' Gina agreed.

'Would you like to keep some of the pieces?' Emily asked, rather tentatively.

'No, thanks, Em. I already have my mother's jewellery collection. Keep it to hand on to your daughter – it might be back in fashion by then!'

'I only hope Gavin and I actually have a daughter – or a son – to pass anything on to,' Emily confided wistfully.

'You will,' Gina said firmly. 'You might even have twins!'

'Just one healthy baby is all we want,' Emily said softly. Gina looked at her, saw the love for Gavin shining from her blue eyes and nodded, satisfied. She wouldn't trust Jack Dawlish an inch, but she trusted Emily not to do anything to hurt Gavin.

Gina turned to face Jack when he began speaking. He had remained standing and exuded confidence, she thought, and it seemed to her that the tension in the room had eased even before he uttered a single word.

'I'm glad to see so many of you here,' he began quietly.

'I realise this is an unsettling time for you all, but I want to assure you that the management is doing everything possible to ensure the company's continued success.'

'But we haven't been working at full capacity for some time,' someone called out. 'And now there's a rumour that we've lost the Carlisle job – is that true?'

'The Carlisle contract is under review,' Jack acknowledged. 'We haven't lost it yet.' The slight smile which accompanied the words gave the definite impression that he had no intention of losing it either!

'But who's in charge?' It was the same man, obviously an elected spokesman. 'Mr Bruce wasn't here last week, nor were you…sir,' he added belatedly, when Jack raised an eyebrow in silent rebuke of the rather belligerent tone of voice. Gina turned indignantly to confront the speaker herself but, to her amazement, Jack leaped quickly to her brother's defence.

'Last week Gavin Bruce had to deal with his father's death and funeral arrangements,' he said sternly. 'Unfortunately, I was away on other business and didn't hear what had happened until I returned to London. However, I'm here now,' he said, as if that were the answer to everything, yet without actually admitting he was in control, Gina noted. 'Gavin's back this week, hard at work, chasing after new and lucrative contracts,' he continued. 'And, of course, we have to convince existing customers, some of whom dealt exclusively with Peter Bruce for many years, that they can expect the same level of efficiency now he that is no longer at the helm.'

'Will there be any redundancies, sir?' The room stilled as one man voiced the fear they all harboured, and Gina found herself waiting as anxiously as the others for Jack to reply.

'I hope not. Right now, I can't promise there won't be

some temporary lay-offs, but I do mean temporary,' he stressed. 'The next few weeks and months will be crucial, and I'm sure I don't need to remind you all that your co-operation in completing and despatching orders on time is vital.' He paused. 'Any more questions?' No one spoke and he nodded. 'Good.'

The canteen slowly emptied as they filed out, and Gina walked over to Jack.

'Thank you for defending Gavin,' she said shyly. He looked at her expressionlessly.

'A united front, remember? I don't think informing the staff of my true opinion of your brother would be particularly helpful. Do you?' She didn't answer, but her dark eyes glowered her dislike of him. Jack sighed and wished he had simply accepted her thanks. 'Do you want a lift back to "The Beeches"?' he asked.

'No,' she said, wondering if she had enough money with her to pay for a cab.

'Don't be childish...' he began, then stopped and raked his fingers through his hair, leaving it boyishly rumpled. 'Please drive home with me,' he smiled warmly. Gina wavered, then capitulated.

'OK. But only because public transport is non-existent around here,' she added and followed him silently to the car. As he flung his briefcase on to the back seat, she realised, far too late, that she should have taken the opportunity of his lunch 'date' with Emily to search the blasted thing for her father's letter. Damn! She was obviously as useless at spying as she was at everything else.

'I'd like to invite Bill Taggart and his wife to dinner one evening this week,' Jack broke the uncomfortable silence to say. 'He's an old gossip, but he knows the textile business inside out and is well-respected, so if he tells everyone at the Leeds Trade Fair next week that Bruce Casuals is on track, others will listen and take note. Can you manage dinner for six at the house, or shall I book a restaurant somewhere?' His tone indicated strong doubts as to her capability.

'Of course I can manage,' she said haughtily. 'Who are the six?'

'The Taggarts…what's his wife's name?' he frowned.

'Ann,' Gina supplied.

'That's it,' he nodded. 'You, me, Gavin and Emily.'

'Oh? Gavin's invited, is he? Despite being as much use to the business as a chocolate teapot? And won't he cramp your style with Emily?'

'Grow up, Gina,' he sounded bored. Pretending a personal interest in Emily had seemed a good idea at the time, but it could backfire on him badly. He needed Gina to be the gracious hostess, not poison the guests. Or him. He also needed her to persuade Gavin to co-operate with the changes that had to be made. She was far less possessive of the company than Gavin, more interested in it becoming profitable again than in who actually ran it. He hoped. 'If you must know, I took Emily to the bank at lunchtime so she could inspect the jewellery she's inherited.'

'And to lunch.'

'And to lunch,' he agreed. He said nothing more, lest she start to think he was over-protesting his innocence, and sensed her silence gradually becoming less hostile.

'Do you have any objection to my using my father's car while I'm here?' she asked casually. Jack suppressed a grin. Very clever. She sells her own vehicle for five thousand pounds and now asks for a free substitute at a time when I need her goodwill! Still…

'Not at all,' he said gravely. 'It is part of the estate

though,' he reminded her. 'Gavin is entitled to half its value.'

'He won't mind if I use it,' she shrugged. 'I'll sell it and split the proceeds when I have your permission to return to my home in London,' she added pointedly. Jack let it pass. He was sorely tempted to give his 'permission' right now. Gina Bruce was already proving too much of a distraction – hence his offer to move to a hotel, despite the inconvenience that would entail. The kisses they had shared had occupied his thoughts all day, and he could still feel the sensation of holding her soft, pliant body in his arms. Pulling up outside the house, he decided on a compromise which would, hopefully, solve his problem.

'I think it would be better if I move into one of the guest rooms in the other wing,' he said neutrally, and a glimpse of Gina's slender thigh as she climbed out of the car confirmed he was doing the right thing. 'I'll probably be working late most evenings and I wouldn't want to wake you when I come up to bed,' he explained, acutely aware of the blatant lie. He would love to wake her and keep her awake for the rest of the night...

'OK,' Gina shrugged indifferently, and walked ahead of him into the house. Phew! That was an improvement. She wouldn't have to worry he might be contacting Emily as she would if he was in a hotel, yet the house was so big she would be able to pretend he wasn't even there.

If Mary was surprised by Jack's request for a change of room, she hid it well and she and Gina made up the bed in the guest room as far away as possible from Gina's own.

'Your bathroom's next door,' Gina told him when he came in and dumped a holdall on the chair. 'And you get sea views from here,' she added. Jack nodded, sparing the panoramic view a brief glance.

'Fine,' he said tersely. Sea views? As opposed to lingerie-clad Gina Bruce views? No contest, he thought, hanging up several suits in the wardrobe before going to transfer the rest of his belongings, and wondering if he was certifiable for actually suggesting the move.

Gina was about to leave the room when, out of the corner of one eye, she spotted an envelope tucked into the inside pocket of one of his jackets. She stared at it for a moment, her heart beginning to thud painfully. Was that the letter Gavin desperately wanted to read? The letter that might explain why their father had acted as he had? She stood rooted to the spot, her mouth dry with terror at the very thought of what she was contemplating. But this was a perfect opportunity – Mary had returned downstairs and Jack was out of the room – yet she couldn't do it. She silently berated herself for being such a coward, then reminded herself that Gavin needed her to do this. In fact, hadn't she assured him of her help?

She took a deep breath and tried to force her feet to move the necessary steps forwards to enable her to pluck the envelope from the pocket, but they seemed glued to the carpet. It isn't stealing – you can take it, read it, and replace it, without Jack ever knowing, whispered the devil on her shoulder. Still, Gina continued to stand and stare, unable to either move away from temptation or to yield to it.

She was so intent on her inner turmoil that she didn't hear Jack's approaching footsteps when he returned. He was surprised to find her still in the room, and even more surprised by her fixed stare and pale face. She looked as if she had seen a ghost! He followed her gaze and quickly realised what was going on. Or rather, not going on, since she seemed to have resisted the urge to sneak a look at his letter. He was strangely glad about that – not that it would have mattered if she had read it. It wasn't the one she – or, more likely, Gavin – wanted to see.

Jack reached past her and plucked the envelope out of his pocket, nearly giving Gina a heart attack in the process since she hadn't known he was in the room until that moment. She visibly jumped, put a hand to her mouth and stared at him, a guilty flush staining her cheeks. Jack waved the envelope in front of her face, and she saw at once that it wasn't the handwritten one Mr Williams had handed over at the reading of the will. The name and address were typewritten and the envelope bore a post-mark.

'It's from my stockbroker,' Jack informed her, mildly enough. 'Still want to read it?'

'I…I wasn't…' she began to protest, swallowing nervously.

'Don't lie to me,' he interrupted harshly. 'Whatever your father confided to me, either in person or by letter, is strictly private. You didn't really think I'd leave his letter lying around for you or Gavin to get your hands on, did you?' he added. Gina hung her head and wished the floor would open up and swallow her whole. And why did the phone never ring when you wanted it to? she thought, recalling the unwelcome intrusion that morning. Unwelcome? Of course it hadn't been unwelcome! She had never been more relieved to be interrupted. Never! she insisted to a part of her that seemed to be jeering at her. She stole a look at Jack's stern features and wondered if it had been a different man who had held her and kissed her and…stop it!

'I'm sorry,' she said quietly. He nodded tersely in acceptance of her apology and acknowledgement of guilt. Well, guilty in thought, if not in deed. 'I'm going to shower and change before dinner,' she said next, and walked with as much dignity as she could muster out of the room. She half-expected him to stop her, to tell her again how worthless a human being she was, but he said nothing more. Lecture over, apparently.

As soon as she reached the privacy of her own room, she called Gavin on his mobile and told him what had happened.

'I warned you to be careful!' he exclaimed. 'We'll never find it now he's on his guard,' he added with a sigh. Gina was relieved he had given up on that particular plan. She had a feeling Jack Dawlish was one step ahead of them, guessing what they would do even before it had occurred to them. Forewarned by their father probably. Her relief was short-lived.

'He seems to quite like Emily,' Gavin mused. 'Maybe she would have better luck worming information out of him.'

'I don't think that's a good idea, Gav,' she said quickly.

'Why not? She told me he took her to lunch after they'd been to the bank, and was quite friendly.' I bet he was, Gina thought grimly. She hesitated, unsure whether she should tell him of her, probably unfounded, suspicions. The situation between the two men was already quite bad enough – she could be making it far worse for no valid reason. No, for now, she would simply watch very, very closely.

'No disrespect to Emily, but she's no match for Jack Dawlish – none of us is. He's more likely to use her than allow her to use him,' she pointed out. That was as much warning as she cared to give. 'I think she should keep her distance.'

'You're probably right,' he agreed. 'And take your own advice – you stay away from him as well! Listen, I've gotta go now – I'm late for a meeting. I'll talk to you tomorrow,' he said, and disconnected.

Gina showered and dressed, put on make-up to bolster her confidence, but then dithered in her room, unable to summon up the courage to face Jack over dinner. Oh, for God's sake! This is your house, not his! she told herself crossly, and marched downstairs, head held high.

'Ah, there you are.' Mary looked up from the pile of ironing she was tackling and smiled. 'What would you like to eat? Mr Dawlish said an omelette would be fine for him – he's in your father's study, working all evening.' Brilliant, thought Gina, her spirits rising.

'I'll cook it,' she offered. 'But you'll have to take it to him,' she added and, at Mary's raised eyebrow, mumbled, 'We had, um, a bit of a disagreement earlier and I'd rather keep out of his way.'

'I see,' Mary said non-committally. 'I don't mind taking a tray through, and it will be a great help if you pre-pare it.'

'No problem.' Gina moved across to the large pantry which was bigger than the kitchen in her flat. As usual, it was stocked as if preparing to feed an army. Shelves groaned under the weight of tinned and dried goods and there was a massive fridge and a huge chest freezer. 'Will omelette suit you too?' Gina called.

'Lovely.'

'Cheese and ham?' Gina suggested, reaching to add them to the box of eggs she had already picked up.

'Mm, lovely,' Mary said again. Like most people whose job included cooking on an almost daily basis, she thor-oughly enjoyed the occasions when someone catered for her. She had taught Gina the basics, but had to concede the pupil had outstripped the teacher since Gina's return from her finishing school. Mary made no apology for being excellent at plain, English cooking, and working for

Peter Bruce hadn't required her to expand her skills. But Gina could turn her hand to Italian or French cuisine, even Tex-Mex – whatever that might be, Mary thought. She didn't particularly want to find out – pizza was quite exotic enough for her, thank you!

Gina prepared a salad and sliced a crusty loaf to accompany the omelettes and, finding a lemon meringue pie in the fridge, cut a slice for Jack.

'It's about ready,' she told Mary, checking the nicely browned omelette.

'Good timing,' Mary switched off the iron, the task finished, and moved towards Gina. 'Why don't you take the tray yourself?' she suggested impulsively. She didn't know the ins and outs of Jack Dawlish's involvement in the twins' lives, but was well aware of the tension between them. And there had been more than enough of that while Mr Bruce was alive! 'Clear the air – he can't be cross with you, not now you've cooked his supper.'

'Want to bet? Anyway, don't tell him I cooked it – he'll think I put arsenic in it,' she said, firmly pushing the tray into Mary's hands. A sentiment shared by Jasper apparently, she thought, unable to tempt the cat with morsels of chopped ham.

She and Mary ate at the kitchen table, chatting easily as always. Gina began to relax – with Jack safely in the study, it was easy to ignore his presence in the house – and was regaling Mary with somewhat exaggerated stories of her and Sophie's antics while out clubbing when Jack appeared with his empty tray. In a trice, the animation drained from Gina's face, as Mary noted anxiously. She noted, too, Jack's grim expression.

'Coffee, sir?' she asked quickly. Gina snorted at the 'sir' and resolved to tell Mary it wasn't necessary – he hadn't been knighted, had he? Jack's brief glance showed he had heard, but he ignored her and smiled at Mary, his features brightening.

'Yes please. And thank you for the omelette – it was delicious,' he said sincerely.

'Oh, don't thank me. Gina cooked it,' Mary beamed proudly.

'Really?' Jack sounded insultingly amazed. He was surprised, but only because he would have thought she would have refused to prepare him so much as a drink of water, not because he doubted her capability. But Gina stiffened angrily at his tone.

'I told you I could cook,' she reminded him coldly. 'But feel free to go and have your stomach pumped out! In fact, I'll come and watch – there's nothing on TV tonight,' she added. Mary winced at the vitriolic tone, but Jack seemed neither to notice nor care.

'Sorry to disappoint you, I don't have the time to spare,' he said evenly. He took the coffee Mary had hastily poured out and returned to the study, wishing he hadn't overheard Gina giggling over her conquests in London. No doubt, when she next met up with Sophie Allinson, his pass at her would be the subject of further laughter and scorn.

He sighed and pushed her, with difficulty, from his thoughts, turning his attention back to his work. Being in Falworth was playing havoc with his other commitments despite delegating as much as possible to his staff, and there was a meeting in London on Tuesday afternoon that he simply had to attend.

He phoned his assistants, checking on the day's events. There was a list of messages and requests for him to return calls that kept him busy for most of the evening. When he finally felt he had caught up, he leaned back in his chair and tiredly massaged the back of his neck. Absently, he reached for the dregs of the coffee and almost spat it out in revulsion. It was stone cold. He went in search of a fresh brew and found Gina still in the kitchen, busy at the stove. As she had been for some time, he thought, taking in the trays of sweets which were, presumably, all her own work for there was no sign of Mary.

'Thinking of opening a sweet shop?' he asked. Gina looked up briefly from the saucepan, then continued stirring the contents. She and her mother had made sweets together when Gavin was off playing football or following some other male pursuit from which she had been excluded. She was too conscious of her figure to eat much confectionary these days, but making fudge or chocolate relaxed her when she was upset.

'I suppose I have made rather a lot,' she said, 'but Gavin will eat the truffles and coconut ice, and Mary likes fudge.'

'Where is Mary?'

'At the cinema,' Gina told him. A short, tense silence followed in which they both realised they were alone in the house. Jack cleared his throat.

'I came for more coffee, and to tell you the Taggarts are coming to dinner on Wednesday. Eight o' clock – is that OK?'

'Fine,' she nodded, and pointed to the fresh coffee she had made a short time before.

'Thanks.' Jack helped himself. 'You?'

'No, I'll be awake all night if I have any more,' she said, which set Jack's thoughts on a path he had determined he wouldn't tread again.

'There's one more thing,' he perched on the edge of the table, and checked out the array of confectionary while he tried to remember what else he had wanted her for. Besides that, Dawlish! Get your mind above waist level! he rebuked himself. 'What flavour is this fudge?' he asked. Gina glanced up and pointed with her spoon.

'That's rum and raisin and that's coffee and walnut,' she told him.

'May I...?' his hand hovered over the trays.

'Help yourself.' She bit back the added comment that he might as well, since he had helped himself to everything else!

Jack munched contentedly for some minutes, sampling most of her produce. He declared the coffee and walnut fudge the winner, and finally remembered the second matter he had wanted to discuss.

'As you probably know, this house has to be valued for probate purposes. The estate agent is coming tomorrow afternoon at three, but I have to be in London then, so I'd like you to be here to show him around.'

'OK,' she shrugged. 'If you're sure you don't want me at the factory, painting the grass a brighter green or something,' she sniffed. Jack hid a grin.

'Don't tempt me,' he said lightly. He refilled his cup and returned once more to the study. Getting back to work took more of an effort than usual. He told himself it was because he was tired, spreading himself too thinly, but he knew his reluctance to continue working owed more to his enjoyment of sparring with Gina Bruce.

chapter five

Jack had already left for the factory when Gina entered the kitchen in search of coffee on Tuesday morning, Mary told her, handing over the keys to her father's Volvo.

'Did he leave me any orders?' Gina enquired.

'Not exactly, but I gained the distinct impression that he expects to see you at the office. Soon,' Mary added, glancing at her watch. Gina grimaced.

'Oh God,' she muttered. She had hoped organising and shopping for the dinner party, plus dealing with the estate agent, would constitute a day's work. Obviously not. She gulped down coffee and headed for the door. 'See you later.'

She had driven her father's car several times before, but always with him as a passenger, and it seemed weird to be driving it now. It still smelt faintly of his pipe tobacco and she half-expected to hear his voice giving directions she didn't need, or a gruff command to slow down.

Although it was a beautiful, sunny morning, she felt a distinct chill and told herself firmly that it was only because the car had been standing, unused, in the cold garage for some time. She still hopped out quickly when she arrived at the factory, and rubbed at the gooseflesh which had sprung up on her bare arms.

The painters were there, she was pleased to note. They hadn't actually begun working yet, but then neither had she, she thought, as she entered the building. She hoped Jack didn't expect her to stand over them and crack the whip – after all, that was his area of expertise! His orders to her had been to organise the refurbishment, and it was organised.

'Hi, Emily,' she smiled at her sister-in-law. 'Has Jack told you about dinner with the Taggarts tomorrow?'

'Yes,' Emily nodded. 'And I've told Gavin.'

'He is going to come?' Gina asked anxiously.

'Yes, although he isn't awfully pleased about Jack telling him how to spend his evenings. But he wants to be there to fight his corner – he said he doesn't want Bill Taggart to think Jack Dawlish is running the place.'

'We're supposed to be presenting a united front, so I doubt Jack will be throwing his weight about,' Gina said slowly. 'Perhaps I should have a word with Gavin.'

'Yes, you do that. He'll listen to you,' Emily said rather waspishly, but Gina didn't notice her tone. She was silently debating whether to also speak to Jack. She decided she would, and went immediately to his office. If nothing else, it would prove to him she was on the premises.

'Yes, Gina?' he looked up briefly, sounding distracted, then turned his attention back to the document in front of him.

'It's nothing really, it's just…tomorrow night, with the Taggarts.' She was trying to find tactful words for what she wanted to say. 'Butt out' wouldn't, she felt, do the trick.

'Yes?' Jack gave her his full attention. 'Problem?'

'No, not at all,' she denied quickly. 'I wondered if you would mind, well, taking a back seat and letting Gavin play host?' she asked rather tentatively. Jack smiled, relieved that was all that was troubling her.

'I'd already decided to do just that,' he told her. 'The name of the company is Bruce, and the object of the exercise is to restore confidence in that name, not in mine. As far as outsiders are concerned, I'm just here as the financial advisor. Try and convince Gavin it's in his own interests to behave responsibly, Gina. A good word from Bill Taggart will be more effective than a nationwide advertising campaign.'

'Yes, I realise that,' she nodded. Bill Taggart was well known and well liked in the trade. He had started small, with a single market stall, but had expanded rapidly over the years and now had store outlets in all the south coast resorts selling beachwear and sports clothes – most of which were produced by Bruce Casuals. Bill was something of a character. He had kept on his market stalls and occasionally returned to his roots, selling his wares and enjoying the banter of the markets. He had bought from Bruce Casuals for almost forty years – if, he said, the company was sound and continued to place orders with them, many others would follow suit. 'And so does Gavin,' she added, in a we-don't-need-you-to-tell-us tone. Jack pretended not to notice the edge in her voice.

'Good,' he said mildly. 'You haven't forgotten about the estate agent, have you? His name's Fowler, incidentally.'

'Of course I haven't forgotten. Three o'clock at the house,' Gina said impatiently, fed up with his constant lack of confidence in her ability to do anything. Correction – it was her father's lack of confidence, of course, and that was why it hurt. Jack Dawlish didn't know her, he only knew what he had gleaned from her father.

'I'll be leaving shortly and I won't be back until tomorrow morning. Miss Pettit has a contact number if you need me,' he said briskly.

'I doubt that,' Gina muttered.

'I see the painters are here,' Jack continued as if she hadn't spoken. 'Did you arrange for the grounds to be tidied up? They give a bad initial impression.'

'Sure,' she said non-committally, her face impassive. She hoped. Oh no – she'd forgotten about the stupid gardens!

As soon as she was ensconced in the safety of Gavin's office with the door shut, she reached for the 'Yellow Pages' and feverishly dialled the numbers of several contract gardeners. Bruce Casuals employed a full-time gardener-cum-caretaker but, at this time of the year, the grounds were too big for one person to keep tidy. She figured Jack wouldn't want to hire another permanent employee, so the freelance gardeners were the ideal solution. If they came once and blitzed the place, Harry would then be able to maintain it in good order.

When that task was done, she settled down to working out menus and the shopping list for the dinner party. She could have done it more easily at home, of course, with her recipe books to hand, but decided not to antagonise Jack by leaving the factory.

She was glad she had stayed when he poked his head round the door half-an-hour later. He seemed surprised to see her scribbling away, she thought. She felt sure he was checking up on her.

'I'll see you tomorrow.' He paused, then said, 'Don't bother searching the office or my room at "The Beeches". You won't find anything.' Gina looked at him coldly, but didn't deign to answer – to be honest, she couldn't think of a suitably cutting reply. She craned her neck to watch from the window until his Jaguar swept through the gates and then almost left, but decided to hang about for a while in case he returned on some pretext or other, hoping to catch her bunking off. Really, it was like being back at school!

When she felt she had waited long enough, she set off for the town centre and after her shopping was completed, returned to the house to unload the car. Mary saw her and came out to help carry the bags inside.

'I can change my day off this week, if you like,' she offered. But Gina knew she always went to visit her newly widowed sister on Wednesdays.

'Thanks, but it's not necessary. I'll get as much prepared as I can today. Jack's gone to London, so I don't have to show my face at the office again.'

'I've already given the drawing room and dining room an extra thorough polish,' Mary told her. 'And I'll do the downstairs cloakroom next.'

'Great. Thanks.' Gina checked her watch, decided to grab a quick lunch and then start on preparations for the party before the estate agent showed up.

Derek Fowler arrived promptly at three, and Gina began showing him over the house. They started with the cellar which stretched the entire length and breadth of the house, and which housed her father's extensive wine collection, plus an eclectic assortment of old bikes and rusting garden equipment. Gina began to realise what an enormous task was in store for her and Gavin when they sold the house.

But that was only the beginning. After they had wandered through the downstairs rooms and then the bedrooms, she led the way up a narrow flight of stairs to the attics, one of which had been her and Gavin's play-room, the other a storage area Pickfords would have been pleased to own. The playroom contained masses of toys and books, Gavin's train set – bigger than Richard Branson's – their desks and chairs, a doll's house bigger than Gina's London flat, or so it seemed to her now, as she wondered what on earth they were going to do with it all.

The second room was even more cluttered, with trunks

full of old clothes, discarded furniture and paintings evidently considered no longer suitable for downstairs, yet they hadn't been thrown out. A Tiffany lamp caught Gina's eye and she wondered if it would be safe to use if she changed the plug. It might burn the house down instead, of course, which might actually save a lot of hassle! She tore her thoughts away from arson and insurance policies and smiled rather apologetically at Derek Fowler.

'Um, the house was bought by my grandfather in the 1920s – we seem to be a family of hoarders.'

'I shouldn't worry about it,' he said, looking round him with interest. 'Some of this must be worth a small fortune now – that mahogany bureau, for example. And that *chaise-longue*,' he added. 'I can recommend a firm that won't rip you off – just give me a ring,' he said handing over a business card. 'Whatever you do, don't go to one of the house-clearance boys – they'll tell you it's rubbish and charge you to take it off your hands,' he warned.

'Thanks,' Gina smiled.

'Is the house going on the market?' he asked next. He had been asked to make a valuation by the executors of the will, but knew they were not the new owners of the property.

'Probably,' Gina said after a slight hesitation. She couldn't bring herself to say a definite 'yes', and she certainly couldn't ask how much money she and Gavin could hope to receive from the sale. It was stupid, of course it was, but she couldn't help the way she felt. Perhaps it was all these reminders of just how long the Bruces had lived here – and still did, in a way, with their possessions cluttering up the place – but she felt uncomfortable discussing the house in terms of hard cash. But Gavin and Emily didn't want to live here, and she certainly didn't. Besides, neither twin could possibly afford to buy out the other's half-share, so of course it would go on the market.

To stiffen her resolve, she left Derek Fowler poking around and returned to the playroom. For once, instead of refusing to remember the night her mother had died, she deliberately let herself recall the events. There had been a furious row between her parents, even louder than usual, and she and Gavin, just ten-years-old, had run up here, placing their hands over their ears to try and shut out the sound of their mother screaming and their father yelling.

There had been a brief silence, then the heavy front door had slammed shut with a force that reverberated throughout the entire house. They had heard the screech of tyres on gravel as their mother had driven off, then there was another long silence, but the twins had stayed where they were until Gavin had whispered that they would be in trouble if they didn't go to bed. So they had crept fearfully downstairs, hugged each other goodnight, and quietly prepared for bed.

Gina had lain awake, listening for the sound of her mother's return. But she never came. Instead, there had been a police car, murmured voices downstairs then, unable to stay in bed any longer, she had gone to wake Gavin and they had sat huddled together on the stairs, shivering with cold and apprehension. Peter Bruce's face, haggard and white, had crumpled when he finally spotted them and he had turned away from the sight of their anxious, pleading eyes. He had always turned away, Gina thought now, both before and after their mother's death and, even now, after his own death, he had favoured an outsider... She turned and went back to Derek Fowler.

'Yes, we'll definitely be selling,' she told him, in a cold, hard voice. 'How much will we get for it?'

'Oh, around a million,' he said airily. 'Can I go and look at the gardens?'

'Sure.' Gina followed him outside feeling rather dazed. A million pounds? The shackles of Jack Dawlish's tyranny had suddenly loosened. But not for Gavin though, she realised quickly, not if he wanted to run the company. And Jack was the executor, they couldn't sell without his agreement. Except that David Williams is also an executor, she remembered.

When Derek Fowler had given her details of his commission rates and promised to come back for more thorough details of the property when she was ready to put it on the market, she showed him out and then promptly phoned the solicitor.

'Yes, Gina, what can I do for you?' he asked, quite genially, she noted gladly. She had been afraid he might be offended after Gavin's outburst at the reading of the will.

'I wanted to ask you how soon Gavin and I can put "The Beeches" on the market.'

'As soon as you wish, but it can't actually be sold until the estate is settled,' he warned. 'You would have to make that clear to any prospective buyer.'

'Oh. And when will that be?' she asked and heard him sigh.

'That depends on Gavin. If he persists in contesting the will…well, it could drag on for months.'

'He hasn't mentioned that again,' she assured him quickly. 'He was angry, shocked. I know he's spoken to the accountant since, and I think he's accepted there's nothing he can do about Jack Dawlish taking control of the company.'

'Good. Then everything should be fairly straightforward. Has the house been valued?'

'Yes. Apparently we can expect around a million pounds,' she told him.

'Mm. You do realise you'll be liable for capital gains tax?' he asked. Damn! Gina thought, but refused to admit her ignorance.

'Yes, I know,' she said airily. 'Mr Williams…can I ask you something else?'

'You may ask,' he said cautiously, 'but I might not be able to answer.'

'I just wondered…do you understand why Dad changed his will? Didn't he realise how hurt Gavin would be?'

'That's two questions,' he commented dryly, hesitated, and then said, 'I'm not an accountant, Gina, but it's my understanding the company was – is – in financial trouble. Your father trusted Jack Dawlish to turn it around.'

'He didn't trust Gavin?' She didn't expect or receive an answer to that. 'Forget I asked.'

'I know you and Gavin never had an easy relationship with your father,' David Williams said slowly, 'but he always looked after you financially. I'm sure he did what he thought was necessary to ensure that continued after his death.'

'Yes, OK,' Gina sighed. Surely there had been another way? One which wouldn't have wounded Gavin so deeply? 'Thanks for talking to me.'

'Not at all, my pleasure,' he said gallantly. 'Goodbye dear.'

'You might have warned me you were driving Dad's car,' Gavin grumbled when he arrived early that evening. 'It gave me quite a turn, seeing it parked in the driveway!'

'Hello to you too,' Gina responded. 'Coffee?'

'No, thanks,' he declined, but followed her into the kitchen. 'Is it right what I hear – that Dawlish is in London overnight?' he asked eagerly.

'Yes...no, Gavin! We are not searching his room!' Gina said in some alarm, correctly reading the gleam in his eye. 'It would be useless anyhow. He made a point of telling me he hadn't left anything of interest lying around.'

'OK, I'll not go in *his* room,' Gavin said edgily, still infuriated that the man had the gall to stay at the house. 'But I'm pretty sure there's no law says I can't go into the study of what is actually my house.'

'Our house,' Gina corrected mildly, and tried to divert him from his purpose by telling him about the estate agent's visit.

'Half a million each,' Gavin mused. 'Less tax, of course. Don't plan a shopping spree just yet,' he warned.

'I know we have to pay capital gains tax,' she said loftily. Gavin wasn't fooled. He grinned.

'Who told you about that?'

'Mr Williams,' she admitted. 'How much will we have to pay?'

'I'm not too sure. A part, a small part, will be tax-free. Above that limit, we'll have to pay forty per cent,' he told her. Gina grimaced. That much?

'There's loads of stuff in the attic that I'd forgotten about. Do you want to come and look?' She had been dying to go back and rummage, but not alone, for she was still edgy after the memories that had flooded back that afternoon. But Gavin shook his head.

'Not tonight, I'm going to check out the study while the coast is clear,' he said stubbornly.

'Oh, Gavin,' Gina sighed, then got to her feet. 'Well, I want no part of it. I'm going for a walk on the beach.'

'Suit yourself.'

She knew he was annoyed by her lack of co-operation and, as always when at odds with him, she felt low in spirits as she left the house. The gate at the bottom of the garden had to be kept locked – unless they wished to open up the house and grounds to holidaymakers and sell tea and sandwiches – and it took her some time to turn the key in the rusting lock. Evidently, no one had been this way for a while, probably not since last summer.

Finally she succeeded, and opened the gate which led out on to the path running along the cliff top. From the path, stone steps led down to the beach and Gina ran down them, trying to empty her head of troublesome thoughts and simply listen to the sounds of waves breaking on the shore, and the screech of seagulls overhead.

It was too early in the year for the resort to be packed with tourists, and those who preferred to visit out of season had already returned to their hotels and guest-houses, so the beach was almost empty. She walked briskly, enjoying the cool wind off the sea which buffeted her, whipping her hair around her face.

'Gina!' She spun round, startled, when she heard her name called. A blond guy of around thirty loped towards her, a golden Labrador at his heels. It was the dog that jolted her memory. Of course, Steve Forrest, the local vet, and Holly. Holly was always at the surgery, seemingly a calming influence on the patients, as if she were somehow able to tell them there was nothing to worry about.

'Hi, Steve,' she greeted him.

'Oh, good, you do recognise me then?' he grinned, coming to a halt beside her. For a moment, he had been afraid she wouldn't have known who he was. Steve saw Gavin Bruce quite often at the rugby club where they both played – and drank – but he didn't see nearly enough of Gavin's gorgeous twin. 'I heard about your dad. I'm sorry.'

'Thanks,' Gina smiled briefly, then turned away and

bent to make a fuss of Holly who was nudging at her hand for attention. She gave the dog another pat and then continued walking. Steve fell in to step beside her.

'Is that why you're down here?' he asked.

'Mm, there's a lot to sort out,' she said vaguely.

'I can imagine,' he paused and cleared his throat. 'I'd like to see you before you go back to London…'

'Actually, I am worried about Jasper – our cat,' Gina interrupted quickly. Gavin had teased her about Steve's continual oh-so-casual enquiries as to when she would be visiting Fulworth. This was a complication she could do without. The cat? It wasn't what Steve had in mind, but it would suffice. For starters.

'What's wrong with him?'

'Probably just old age, but he's off his food which is unlike him, and he seems a bit miserable,' she told him.

'I'm at a seminar tomorrow, but bring him in to the surgery on Thursday morning and I'll check him over, maybe do some tests,' Steve said.

'I will, thanks,' she smiled gratefully. They continued walking, throwing sticks for Holly to retrieve, and chatting idly until they neared the pier. A rowdy group of youths had gathered, drinking and shouting obscene suggestions to another group of teenage girls. Not that the giggling girls seemed to object, Steve noted, thankful that he needn't intervene. They were only boys, true, but there were six of them, their courage fuelled by alcohol, and he would hate to make a fool of himself in front of Gina Bruce. She grimaced in distaste at the remarks, her quiet stroll spoiled, and turned to face the way she had come.

'I think I'll go back.'

'I'll walk with you – it's getting dark,' Steve said, whistling for Holly to come to heel. Gina seemed to neither welcome nor resent his presence, and he toyed

with the idea of inviting her out. Minus the cat. Losing his
nerve, he decided to ask Gavin to arrange a double date.
'Isn't that your house?' he pointed. 'Some lights have just
been switched on – I hope you aren't being burgled.'

'Do burglars turn the lights on?' Gina asked lightly, then
as she realised the lighted upstairs room was Jack's,
gasped in dismay. Gavin shouldn't be up there! OK, he
had a point about the study being neutral territory, as it
were, but not Jack's room, particularly now he could no
longer be considered an uninvited guest. He had offered
to move to a hotel, and she had told him not to. Therefore,
he was entitled to the same privacy the family would
afford any other guest. It was a pity she had omitted to
actually tell Gavin about Jack's offer to move out, of
course, but she couldn't tell him without giving her reason
for acting as she had.

'Do you have a mobile phone with you?' she asked
Steve.

'Sure.' Steve always carried one, in case he was needed
in an emergency, and unclipped it from his belt and
handed it over. Gina punched out the number for "The
Beeches".

'Gavin, you idiot! I told you...' she began furiously.

'Gina? Is that you?' It was Jack's voice, and Gina gave
a yelp of horror, almost dropping the phone in her agitation. He was supposed to be in London! Was Gavin still
there? Had he been caught red-handed? Was he dead? Oh,
get a grip girl, she admonished herself, and took a deep,
steadying breath. She considered simply disconnecting,
but figured that would be cowardly. Not to mention futile,
since he had recognised her voice. 'Gina?'

'Yes. Sorry, bad connection,' she fibbed, then realising
attack was the best form of defence, continued crossly,
'You frightened me! You said you wouldn't be back

tonight and Mary's already gone to her sister's, so when I saw the lights go on in the house, I thought it must be Gavin. Hoped it was, anyway, otherwise I was going to call the police,' she babbled, hoping he would accept that her agitation stemmed from fear of burglars. Actually, considering her state of near panic, she was quite pleased with her tirade, feeling that she had rationally explained away her assumption that it was Gavin who had answered the phone. As long as Gavin wasn't still at the house, there was no reason for Jack to know he had been there at all that evening.

'I'm sorry I startled you. I decided to get back for an early start tomorrow morning,' Jack said, which wasn't strictly true. He had told himself he should get back to Falworth to see what mischief the twins were up to in his absence, which was valid enough, but not the whole reason for his decision to drive back. His London house had seemed lonely and empty, yet there had been no one whose company he had craved. Not in London anyhow. 'Where are you ringing from?' he asked, wondering how she had spotted him turning on lights at the rear of the house.

'On the beach. Don't lock the garden gate or I'll have a very long walk round by road,' she said.

'OK.' He certainly sounded calm, Gina thought, not at all as if he had found Gavin snooping, but she hurried anyway, silently cursing the soft sand that hampered her footsteps. Finally, she reached the steps and started up them. She had completely forgotten Steve Forrest, who had followed in her wake, hoping for an invitation to coffee. Or something.

'Gina?'

'Yes?' she turned impatiently. He wanted to ask if it was her boyfriend she was rushing to meet, but didn't want to hear the reply. She was certainly in a hurry to see someone. Playing it cool, he grinned – winsomely, he hoped – and asked, 'Can I have my mobile back please?'

'Oh! Sorry!' Gina laughed and tossed it down to him. 'Thanks. And I'll see you on Thursday,' she called over her shoulder as she turned and began running up towards the gate.

'I'll look forward to it,' Steve called back. Jack, having decided that a stroll on the beach with Gina would be an excellent way to unwind after a gruelling day, stopped dead in his tracks when he heard the exchange. Then he quietly pulled open the gate and peered out to get a look at the man she had arranged a date with. A blond guy with a golden Labrador…who on earth was that?

'Oh, my God!' Gina almost fell back down the steps when Jack loomed up in front of her. Was he determined to give her heart failure? Jack reached out and, grabbing her wrist, hauled her none too gently to the safety of the garden. 'Are you actually trying to scare me witless?' she grumbled, turning to lock the gate behind them.

'Of course not,' he forced a smile, reminding himself that it was none of his business who she dated. She was free to go out with anyone she cared to on Thursday evening…unless he arranged to entertain clients, he thought, mentally reviewing the list of people who needed convincing of the soundness of Bruce Casuals. He pushed aside the thought as being unworthy of him and hardly in keeping with his resolve to keep his distance from the temptation of Gina Bruce.

'You look tired,' Gina commented when they were inside the brightly lit kitchen. Indeed, dark circles shadowed his eyes and there were lines of strain etched deep around his mouth. And you look gorgeous, Jack thought. The walk along the beach had whipped colour into her cheeks and tousled her glossy hair...or was the blond beach bum responsible for her dishevelled state?

'I've had a bad day,' he said shortly. And it was getting worse, not better as he had hoped when he set out from London.

'Can I get you something to eat?' Gina asked, aware she was consorting with the enemy, but unable to stop herself when he seemed so weary. Besides, she *had* insisted he stay, so she could no longer treat him as if he were an interloper.

'No. Thank you,' he belatedly remembered his manners. Gina frowned slightly. Was he merely tired? Or angry? she wondered uneasily.

'Coffee?' she ventured, eyeing him warily. He shook his head.

'No, I'm going to bed. Will you lock up? Or leave a note for Mary if she isn't back by the time you want to go up?' he added, remembering she had told him Mary was out.

'Sure,' Gina nodded, and didn't explain that Mary wouldn't be back at all that night.

'Oh...how did it go with the estate agent?' Jack paused to ask.

'Fine. He's putting a written valuation in the post to you, but he said Gavin and I could sell for around a million pounds,' she told him.

'Good.' He continued on his way, then paused again and glanced back at her. 'Don't count your chickens though, Gina. There aren't many people who can afford that sort of money,' he cautioned 'you might have to wait quite a while for a buyer. And then you'll have to pay capital gains tax,' he added, thinking he was helping and there-fore completely taken aback by her reaction.

'Oh, for Heaven's sake! What is it with you men and

capital gains tax!' she fumed, thoroughly exasperated. First, Mr Williams, then Gavin, and now Jack! 'I'm fully expecting to receive a letter tomorrow, personally signed by the Chancellor of the Exchequer, reminding me of my obligations!'

'What did I say?' Jack asked, bemused by her outburst.

'Oh, nothing. I thought you were going to bed!' she snapped.

'Come with me,' he said. He hadn't meant to say it out loud and cursed his tiredness and his ridiculous decision to drive back tonight when it would have made far more sense to stay in London overnight. They stared at each other for a long, tense moment and Gina's heart began to pound heavily. Her treacherous body began to ache with remembered delight caused by his kisses, his hands on her skin, her breasts...her nipples hardened in anticipation and she crossed her arms defensively over her chest.

'What?' she whispered.

'To the study,' Jack's overtired brain ticked over slowly as he sought desperately to retrieve the situation. 'I want to check on something and I want you to come with me,' he said more convincingly.

'The study? You want me to come with you to the study?' Gina queried slowly.

'That's what I just said. Isn't it?'

'Er, yes.' Telling herself she was relieved, not disappointed, she trailed after him to her father's study. 'What are we looking at?' she asked, as he snapped on the light but stopped on the threshold of the room.

'That,' he pointed to the closed filing cabinet.

'What about it?'

'I purposely left one drawer open, just half-an-inch. They're all closed now,' he told her. 'Who's been in here, Gina?' he asked softly. 'You? Or your brother?'

'I haven't touched anything,' she said and met his gaze squarely.

'And Gavin? Has he been here this evening?' Jack's steel-grey eyes bore into hers. Gina shrugged.

'I've been on the beach.'

'So you have,' Jack agreed, too weary in mind and body to spar with her further. 'Goodnight, Gina.'

'Goodnight,' she echoed, and watched as he slowly climbed the stairs. She felt unaccountably guilty, as if she and Gavin were responsible for his obvious exhaustion, and had to remind herself that they hadn't asked him to take over their lives.

She made coffee for herself and sat watching TV for a while, but she couldn't shake off the feeling of guilt. She flicked through the channels restlessly – a habit which enraged her in other people – but could find nothing to hold her attention. It wasn't even ten o' clock when she secured the house for the night and went to bed. She paused at the top of the stairs and looked along the darkened hall to the left. No light showed from beneath Jack's door and she turned right to her own room. It was a long time before she slept.

'Where's Mary?'

'It's her day off,' Gina looked up briefly from the soft fruit she was sorting through. Jack frowned.

'I assumed she would be here to help you with the dinner party,' he said.

'Well, she isn't,' Gina responded rather shortly. Here we go again. The Gina's-too-useless-to-cope speech, she thought irritably. 'You'll have to get your own breakfast,' she told him by way of revenge.

'I'm not hungry.' Jack moved to pour coffee from a still-steaming pot. 'Do you want Emily to come and give you a hand?'

'No!' Gina bit out.

'I'm only trying to help,' he said mildly. Gina took a deep breath and faced him, hands belligerently on hips, dark eyes flashing sparks.

'I do not need help. Not yours, not Mary's, not Emily's. OK?'

'Fine,' Jack agreed, hiding a smile. He guessed telling her she was beautiful when she was angry would only add fuel to the fire, so he desisted. But she was!

He wandered over to the open window and glanced out, admiring the expanse of lawn and flower beds which sloped down to the cliff top, the distant view of the sea, sparkling in the sunshine. It was a peaceful scene, unlike London. He was suddenly glad that he had driven down the evening before, even though that had resulted in a restless night – either caused by overhearing Gina arranging a date, or by her close proximity – he wasn't sure which. A bit of both probably. He could no longer deny to himself that the bewitching minx was getting under his skin. Too often, his thoughts were occupied with her.

'Idyllic place, this,' he commented. Gina spared a brief glance for the view. She had grown up with it and took it for granted. On balance, she thought she preferred London.

'It is lovely at this time of the year,' she agreed. 'But it's desolate in winter and too crowded in the school summer holidays. That's why we keep the garden door locked – holidaymakers kept wandering in and expecting tea and sandwiches!'

'I bet that pleased your father,' Jack commented dryly. A more private man than Peter Bruce he had yet to meet.

'Mm. Sometimes, if he was out, I would provide refreshments and charge a fiver per person!' she confessed. Jack's grin broadened.

'An entrepreneur, after all. You're full of surprises,' he told her. He helped himself to more coffee and glanced at his watch. He ought to be leaving but was reluctant to do so. In fact, he wished he could take the whole day off, walk along the cliff, take a boat out…he was jolted out of his reverie by the realisation that he was imagining having Gina's company as he played truant.

'The sight of all that food is making me feel hungry,' he decided.

'You'll find orange juice, milk, butter and eggs in the fridge,' Gina said briskly without looking up. She was damned if she was going to prepare his breakfast. 'There's cereal on the shelf to your right as you go in the pantry and the bread's already by the toaster,' she added.

'What are you making for dinner?' Jack asked a few minutes later, through a mouthful of cornflakes.

'Artichoke and watercress soup with cheesy toasts, then roast lamb – Bill Taggart hates food to be "mucked about" as he calls it,' she explained, lest he think her unadventurous. 'For pudding, lemon syllabub with raspberry puree and cinnamon apple and pear tart with meringue topping. Ann Taggart has a sweet tooth,' she added, rather unnecessarily. Jack's mouth was watering in anticipation.

'Talking of sweets…is there any of that coffee and walnut fudge left?' he asked longingly. Gina smiled and went to fetch it from the tray in the pantry and transferred the slices to a paper bag.

'I managed to buy some small paper cases yesterday, so I'm going to put the rest of the sweets in them to have with coffee and call them *petit fours*,' she told him as she handed over the bag.

'Good idea. Did you keep the receipts for all this food? Don't forget you can claim it on expenses.'

'OK,' she nodded.

'What about the wine?'

'I didn't buy any – there's loads down in the cellar.'

'Do you want me to choose?' he asked.

'If you like. But, unless you're a wine-buff, I wouldn't pick anything vintage. Bill Taggart prefers scotch and Ann adds lemonade to everything.'

'Everything?' Jack raised an eyebrow.

'Everything,' she confirmed, grinning at the expression on his face.

'Plonk for them then,' he muttered as he disappeared down the cellar steps. 'You were right – your father built up an amazing collection,' he said when he emerged clutching four dusty bottles. He began to sneeze after being in the musty cellar and moved to open the door to the garden to get some fresh air.

'Don't let Jasper in here!' Gina called.

'He's asleep under the hedge,' Jack told her, coming back inside as soon as he'd stopped sneezing. 'Why don't you want him in here? Oh, forget I asked,' he added, gesturing to the food she'd laid out.

'Mm, he's so sneaky,' she said and, as Jack watched her, her lips curved into a slight smile of remembrance.

'What are you thinking about?'

'Oh, just one of his antics. I was catering for Dad, but I'd only made one dessert – individual trifles. I left them uncovered and when I came back in here to carry them through to the dining room, he had licked off all the cream from the top of one. He was still sitting on the worktop, cleaning his whiskers, looking completely pleased with himself! Two of the guests hadn't even been invited, so I was already pretending to be on a diet so that the food would stretch, and I'd used up all the fruit and sponge…but I did have some cream left over,' she looked up at Jack and grinned impishly. He returned the smile.

'Dare I ask who you gave it to? Not your father, I hope?'

'No. Let's just say one of the guests was a creep who kept trying to put his hand up my skirt.'

'Fair enough,' Jack nodded in understanding and agreement, then recalled being accused of assaulting her and wondered if he ought to have been checking his own food for cat hair.

He watched her as she deftly rolled out pastry, her hair escaping from its ponytail and a smudge of flour on her cheek. It was a very domestic scene and he ought to have been scared by how comfortable he felt. It was almost as if they were living together, but without sex. Unfortunately.

Jack had lived with only one of his girlfriends and had decided never to again. Not that it had ended in acrimony, quite the reverse. He still crossed paths with Stella occasionally, as she also worked in the City as a commodities broker and they got along well enough. But they had both realised living together wasn't going to work out when, less than six months into the relationship, they were both back in the habit of taking their briefcases into the bedroom at night, more interested in the next day's workload than in making love. He couldn't imagine wanting to work in bed if Gina Bruce were beside him, and couldn't imagine her putting up with it either! Her passionate response to his kisses and caresses was impossible to forget. If only they had met under different circumstances…he shook his head to clear his thoughts.

'I'm going to the factory,' he said shortly.

'OK. Jack?' she looked up. He paused.

'Yes?'

'Please don't have a go at Gavin about opening the filing cabinet,' she pleaded. 'After all, he might have been looking for…for his birth certificate. Or something.'

'Or something,' he agreed dully. He hesitated then said, 'Very well.'

'Thank you,' she smiled her relief. Rather reluctantly, Jack returned her smile.

'I'll see you later.'

chapter six

When Jack returned at lunchtime, he was immediately aware of the delicious aroma of baking – the cinnamon apple and pear tart, he guessed. The kitchen was empty, however, except for Jasper who was snoozing peacefully in his basket, and the pantry door firmly closed against intruders. The goodies, presumably, safely inside.

'Gina?'

'In here,' she called. He followed the sound of her voice and found her in the conservatory, arranging flowers. 'Checking up on me?' she asked.

'No,' he said truthfully. 'I thought you might like a break – it's a lovely day. We could go for a walk and stop off somewhere for a pub lunch.'

'Is Emily too busy to go?' Gina enquired tartly. Jack stifled a sigh, but he only had himself to blame, after all. 'Of course.' Gina clicked her fingers in sudden understanding. 'Gavin's in the office today, isn't he? He's cramping your style...' She stopped speaking abruptly. She had to, for Jack's mouth was covering hers; his hands gripped her shoulders and pulled her towards him, then slid slowly down her back to rest at her waist. When her shocked surprise gave way to a melting response, Jack forced himself to break the kiss. Gina stared at him, her eyes wide, her lips still parted.

'Well, that was both an effective and pleasant way of shutting you up,' Jack drawled. 'Your jealousy of Emily is flattering but becoming tedious. Not to mention unnecessary,' he added. Gina finally recovered the power of speech.

'J...jealousy?' she spluttered, then said louder, 'Jealousy! You conceited oaf! I couldn't give a toss if you have a million girlfriends! I'm concerned for Gavin, that's all,' she insisted.

'OK, point taken. Stop screeching at me.' Jack was still amused, she felt, and she continued to glower at him. 'Calm down, Gina. Even if I did lust after Emily – which I most certainly do not – I would never pursue a married woman, any married woman,' he emphasised. 'And if you don't believe that, ask yourself why on earth I would risk antagonising Gavin when I need his co-operation to run the company,' he said reasonably.

'Yes, well,' Gina mumbled, unable to think of a more coherent reply. Jealous? Am I? she wondered. When it had first occurred to her that Jack might be interested in Emily, her reaction had been one hundred per cent concern for Gavin. Could she honestly say the same now?

'Put those flowers down and finish them later,' Jack said, then settled the matter by taking them from her hands and placing them back in the tub of cold water with the others. 'I've spent the morning in a stuffy office and you've spent it in the kitchen, so let's get out in the fresh air and go for some lunch – OK?'

'OK,' she agreed finally after mentally reviewing her checklist of things still to be done for the dinner party. All the food was prepared, she only had to lay the table and finish the floral arrangements. Once that was done, she could concentrate on her own appearance.

She was afraid she looked a fright now, in old jeans and T-shirt, her hair scrunched back in a ponytail and no make-up, but she couldn't think of a logical reason to go and smarten herself up. She contented herself with pulling her hair free and combing it with her fingers, and donning sunglasses before they left the house.

By unspoken, mutual agreement they left via the garden gate on to the cliff top. Being there reminded them both, albeit for different reasons, of Gina's meeting with Steve Forrest the night before.

'I want to take Jasper to the vet tomorrow morning,' Gina said. 'I hope that won't be a problem? Or do I need a note from you excusing me from being at the factory?' she asked tartly.

'No,' Jack smiled slightly. 'The dinner party counts as work – I didn't expect you to be at the office bright and early after a late night entertaining clients.' He hesitated, vividly aware of her date with the blond beach bum and, knowing he was being unfair, continued anyway, 'But I'd like you to spare me a couple of hours tomorrow evening.'

'Oh? Why?' Gina asked. She didn't seem overly perturbed by the request, Jack noted, slightly puzzled. Perhaps she was looking for an excuse to cancel the date, or perhaps it was scheduled for next week. He filed that thought away for future consideration – OK, sabotage!

'Miss Pettit is getting together a list of customers who haven't placed any substantial orders with the company for more than a year. I'd like to go through the names with you since you'll probably know most of them. I don't want to incur the expense of entertaining them individually, but I thought a buffet lunch at the factory, followed by a tour showing off new lines might prove worthwhile.'

'Mm. How many for lunch?'

'About twenty, maybe more. I don't really know yet, not until I see the list and the value of past orders. I figure a personal call from you would actually get them here, then it's down to Gavin to sell the wares and for me to convince them that we can fulfil any orders on time.'

'Gavin's at the Trade Fair all next week,' she reminded him. Jack nodded.

'I know. I was planning it for the following week. Hopefully the decorators will have finished by then, and the whole place will project a prosperous new image.'

'Wouldn't they appreciate lunch at the house rather than at the factory?' Gina suggested. 'The canteen's too basic and the boardroom too small.' The grandly named boardroom was in fact a little-used office.

'If you don't mind having a horde of people in the house then yes, it would be better,' Jack agreed. 'But – and don't take this the wrong way – a "for sale" sign outside would give the immediate impression that you and Gavin are strapped for cash.'

'We are,' Gina said promptly, but without rancour. 'I haven't discussed the sale with Gavin yet. There's loads to sort out – we'll keep Pickfords in business for a month,' she added gloomily, thinking of the crowded attics. And she didn't like the idea of hiring strangers to just cart it all off to an auction room or, even worse, a rubbish dump.

'It can still go on the market and be advertised in the press,' Jack told her. 'Just ask the agent to hold off on putting up a board – they're a mixed blessing anyway,' he added, 'you can get a lot of time-wasters who just want to have a look round and have no intention of buying.'

'Ugh,' Gina grimaced slightly. She found the prospect of showing prospective buyers – or sightseers – around her home distinctly unappealing. If Gavin agreed, she thought she would prefer to wait until she was back living in London again, and let the estate agent deal with it all.

'Are you hungry?' Jack slowed as they neared a pub.

'Not really, I've been picking at food all morning,' she confessed. 'only to ensure it's good enough for our guests, of course!'

'Of course,' Jack agreed smiling. 'And I've eaten all that fudge,' he made a confession of his own. 'And Miss Pettit brought me biscuits as well as coffee at eleven.'

'Doesn't your PA in London bring you coffee and biscuits?' she asked. 'I thought that was an important part of the job!' Jack pulled a face.

'You're joking. Decaff coffee, without cream or sugar. She's on a perpetual diet and health-kick and believes in sharing her suffering,' he said ruefully. Gina grinned.

'I expect she has a stash of chocolate biscuits in her desk and is just getting her revenge on you for being yelled at or something...look, those people are leaving,' she pointed to a table being vacated. It was in a sheltered spot against a wall, looking out over the sea.

'Grab it while I get some drinks,' Jack said. 'What would you like?'

'Just orange juice, please. And a ham roll,' she decided.

'OK,' Jack disappeared inside the pub and joined her a few minutes later. He had chosen a cheese and pickle sandwich and a pint of beer for himself, and they ate and drank in silence for a while. It was a lovely day, sunny but not too hot, with a cool breeze coming in off the sea. Quite a lot of people were out on jet-skis, or sailing, skimming across the waves.

'Do you sail?' Jack asked.

'I haven't for awhile, but I know my way round a boat,' she said. 'Gavin used to own one, but Emily hates the sea, so he sold it.'

'Pity. It's a great get-away-from-it-all experience,' Jack commented, rather to her surprise.

'I thought you grew up on a farm?' she asked. And, even with her appalling sense of geography, she knew the Wye valley was nowhere near the sea.

'I did. The parents of a mate at university own a cabin

cruiser. I've spent a few holidays cruising around the south of France and the Greek islands,' he told her.

'It suits me – I can't stand those lie-on-a-beach-and-do-nothing holidays,' he continued. 'I'm bored stiff after a couple of days,' he said before adding casually, 'How about you? What's your favourite holiday?'

Sailing around the Greek islands with you, Gina was appalled to find herself thinking.

'According to you, my whole life's been one long holiday,' she reminded him – and herself – sharply.

Jack sighed. 'I thought – hoped – that we'd called a truce,' he said quite gently, placing a hand over hers. He knew he had been hard on her at first, but he had needed to be. Both she and her brother had to be jolted into the reality of their situation.

Gina couldn't bring herself to jerk her hand away, but left it lying beneath the warmth of his, and looked into his grey eyes, no longer cold and forbidding. And the stern, thin line of his lips…she dropped her gaze to his full mouth, vividly remembering the passion of his kisses…which was the real Jack Dawlish? The cold, unfeeling man her father – similarly cold and unfeeling – had trusted and favoured above his own children, or the sensual man who so easily awakened hitherto unknown desires in her? It was all so confusing. He was undoubtedly doing his utmost to turn Bruce Casuals into a profitable business once more – but for whose benefit? He owned a majority shareholding, after all. Her gut instinct was to trust him, and yet Gavin most emphatically did not. And Gavin had known him for far longer than she had, and had fought against his involvement in the company from the outset. And Gavin was using his head, whereas she was being swamped by…hormones? So, Gavin's brain versus her hormones? No contest. She finished her glass of juice and rose to her feet.

'I'd better get back to work, I've sill got a lot to do this afternoon,' she said coolly.

'OK.' Jack drained his own glass, snatched up the remainder of his sandwich to eat on the way, and fell into step beside her. He had seen the confusion in her stormy eyes and had wanted to kiss away her doubts. But he had resisted the temptation. Kissing Gina Bruce was becoming a habit, one which could, he felt sure, easily become an addiction. Heroin would be safer, he thought grimly. Seducing Peter Bruce's daughter had definitely not been part of the agreement.

The walk back to the house was brisker and more silent than the stroll to the pub. Without saying a word, Gina went straight back to the conservatory to continue with her flower arrangements, and Jack got back into his car and drove back to the factory. On his way to his office, he paused by Miss Pettit's desk.

'Have you got that list of ex-customers ready?'

'No – you said it wasn't urgent,' she raised a questioning brow.

'I know, but I want to go over it with Gina tomorrow,' he replied.

'Get Gina to check the file,' she suggested.

'She doesn't know how to use a computer,' Jack said.

'Of course she does,' Petty exclaimed, then said, 'oh, well, perhaps not.' She belatedly remembered how Gina had asked her to type a memo she was perfectly capable of typing herself. In fact, Gina had plagued the life out of her one school holiday, when Gavin was away playing rugby, to teach her how to use the newly installed computers. She must have her reasons for misleading Jack Dawlish. 'I'll have it ready before you leave today,' she added.

'Thank you,' Jack nodded, and continued on his way, torn between irritation and amusement at Gina's deception. What a stubborn little minx she was! Fortunately for her, amusement won, but he decided not to let her know she had been found out. Not yet, anyway. The knowledge might come in handy one day in the future, he thought.

He dealt with the messages on his desk, then phoned his PA in London to be brought up to speed on what was happening there in his absence. He put Bruce Casuals – and Gina – far from his mind and concentrated on his other clients, delegating as much as possible to his staff. There was only so much they could do though, and he resigned himself to a working weekend in London catching up.

Soon after five, he headed back to "The Beeches", not sure what mood he would find Gina in. The house was silent when he entered and there was no sign of her. Hoping she hadn't fed the Taggarts' dinner to the cat and hastened back to her flat in London, he went through to the kitchen. Several saucepans were on the hob, filled with vegetables and, presumably, waiting to be cooked. Keeping a wary eye on Jasper, he opened the pantry door. The fridge held the finished desserts and a foil-covered roasting pan revealed a large leg of lamb ready for the oven. Phew! Thank goodness for that!

'Sorry Jasper,' he murmured as he closed the pantry door behind him. 'You'll have to make do with leftovers.' But where was Gina? He called her name, but there was no reply. The drawing room was immaculate, two vases filled with fresh flowers adorned occasional tables and scented the air. There was a tray with tiny coffee cups and saucers, plus a covered dish of the sweets, the *petit fours*, awaiting those still hungry after the meal. She had made some peppermint creams to add to those she had made on

Monday evening, he noticed, but he resisted the urge to sample one.

'Gina?' he called again, but still received no response, and so he moved into the dining room. The table bore an exquisitely arranged centrepiece of carnations and roses, the silverware and crystal gleamed, and the neatly folded napkins awaited the diners. Candles in polished silver candlesticks needed only a match to give the room a more intimate glow. Jack felt a stab of compunction for the disparaging remarks he had made about her and Sophie Allinson's catering business. If the food tasted as good as it looked, Gina could quite easily make a success of such a business, and probably already would have done so if she hadn't been cushioned by her father's money. Peter Bruce had thought it reflected badly on a man if his womenfolk had to earn their own living, he remembered. Where on earth was she?

'Gina?' he called again, louder this time, and bounded up the stairs. He hesitated at the top, then walked slowly down the hall towards her room. He was about to call her name again when he heard the sound of music being played in her bathroom. Relief that she hadn't run away after he had unwittingly upset her at lunch, flooded over him. He turned away, then stopped dead when he heard the distinct sound of splashing…she was taking a bath. It took an immense effort of will for him to retrace his steps and go to his own room. No hot bath for him though. A cold shower, a very cold shower, was what he needed!

There was still no sign of Gina when he returned downstairs, and he went to sit out on the terrace to read the newspapers. At one point, he heard sounds of activity in the kitchen, but decided against asking if she required any help. She had told him in no uncertain terms that morning that she did not. And, since then, something had soured the easy companionship they had shared all too briefly at lunchtime. She had definitely distanced herself from him, and he was loath to risk adding fuel to the fire with the Taggarts' imminent arrival.

When he heard a car pull up outside, he put aside his paper and returned indoors. As he walked into the hall, his breath caught in his throat at the sight of Gina. She looked stunning, in tailored black trousers and a gold, satin top, scooped low back and front. Her hair was piled on top of her head, the severe style softened by silky tendrils loose around her temples and neck. Long, dangly, gold earrings were her only jewellery apart from a slim gold watch on one wrist. Spike-heeled, strappy sandals completed a look of utmost elegance and sophistication. So much for cold showers, Jack thought ruefully. All he could think of was how he wanted to drag her off to bed and forget about dinner.

Gina caught him staring at her and stiffened slightly. What had she done wrong now? she wondered, tilting her chin stubbornly and daring him to criticise.

'You...' he swallowed, biting back the words he wanted to say. She was, for some reason, wary of him and for his own self-preservation he had to hide from her just how much he wanted her. And how many times did he have to remind himself of the necessity of maintaining the whip hand over the twins? 'You...scrub up well,' he said lightly, with a slight smile. Luckily, he seemed to have hit the right note. Gina relaxed and grinned back.

'So do you,' she told him. Indeed, he did. He was immaculate in a dark suit, crisp white shirt and a silk grey and blue tie. Gold cufflinks peeked from beneath his cuffs.

'Hi.' It was Gavin who entered first, and he gave Gina

a brief hug. 'The Taggarts are right behind us – they got caught at the traffic lights on The Parade.'

'Oh, right.' Nervously, Gina checked her reflection in the hall mirror, patting at her hair and wishing she had left it loose. 'Gav – can you just fasten the hook and eye on my top?' she asked, turning her back to him. His large fingers fumbled with the intricate fastening and, as Jack noticed for the first time the row of tiny buttons from waist to neck, his fingers itched to trade places with Gavin – only he would be undoing them, not making the top more secure.

'Why do you girls always buy clothes with such fiddly fastenings?' Gavin grumbled.

'To make you men feel inadequate?' Gina suggested, twisting round to grin at him. 'Hello, Emily, you look lovely.'

'Thanks. So do you.' Emily's smile seemed forced. Jack lightly touched her arm.

'Are you OK?'

'Fine,' she said brightly, then she sighed and her shoulders sagged. 'Why is it that whenever I'm at a "do" with Gina, I always manage to get it wrong?' she sighed again. 'Compared to her, I'm either overdressed or underdressed.' She glanced disparagingly down at her full, bright blue taffeta skirt. 'I look like a meringue. A mouldy meringue, at that,' she added glumly.

'Nonsense, you look very pretty,' Jack assured her. 'The colour matches your eyes.' Gina overheard that and gave vent to a disdainful sniff reminiscent of a dowager Duchess at her best.

The Taggarts' Daimler purred to a halt outside the still-open front door, and Gavin and Gina went to greet them. Jack deliberately stayed in the background. He was, after all, only the company's financial adviser so far as Bill

Taggart was concerned. Emily did likewise but, in her case, from shyness.

Bill Taggart was a big bear of a man in his sixties, with a full head of silvering hair and a bushy beard. His wife, Ann, was petite, well groomed, her short bob still blonde with the subtle help of her hair stylist. There was a general flurry of handshakes between the men and air kissing between the women, then Gina suggested they have drinks on the terrace before dinner.

Jack noticed that Bill asked for scotch, just as Gina had said he would, and Ann wanted vodka and lemonade, also as Gina had told him. He caught her eye and smiled slightly.

'We were so sorry to hear about your father,' Ann said to Gina, 'such a shock, though of course he hadn't been well recently, had he? Bill said...' she chattered on, conversing easily with Gina, who was relaxed and at ease with the situation Jack noted. Emily, on the other hand, was patently not comfortable, perched on the edge of her chair, twisting her hands nervously in her lap, and contributing little to the conversation.

'I've been checking up on you, Dawlish,' Bill Taggart suddenly boomed at Jack. He smiled slightly.

'I'd have been surprised if you hadn't,' he responded.

'Word is, you know your stuff. But what's the story with Bruce Casuals? A little out of your usual sphere, isn't it?'

'Not really,' Jack shrugged. 'And there's no story. Peter Bruce could run the company as a one-man show because he had an excellent sales director bringing in the orders,' he inclined his head towards Gavin, who looked surprised but kept silent. 'But Gavin can't be in two places at once,' Jack continued smoothly. 'When Peter became ill, things became a little lax at the office. The company's sound, there was a temporary problem with administration, that's all,' he finished.

'Hm,' Bill regarded him steadily, then turned to Gavin. 'All my shop managers tell me the summer beachwear has been flying out the doors…'

'Oh yes, I bought a matching set,' Ann interrupted. 'Sarongs are so flattering, aren't they? They hide every bulge,' she laughed, confident that for her age she had very few bulges that needed to be concealed. 'Beautiful silk, and such glorious patterns.'

'We get it from a supplier in Hong Kong,' Gavin told her.

'Talking of the Far East…' Bill began. Gina, guessing he was about to compare the cost of sweatshop labour in Asia with the wages paid to British workers, rose to her feet.

'Shall we go in to dinner?' she smiled, and led the way back indoors, telling Gavin to get everyone seated while she dealt with the food. 'Emily, can you take the soup in while I watch these?' Gina shoved the tureen at her sister-in-law, while keeping her eye on the cheese toasts browning under the grill. As soon as the cheese topping bubbled and browned, she whisked them out, cut them into small squares and placed them on individual plates to accompany the soup. Before following Emily into the dining room, she quickly checked on the roast and the vegetables, and nodded in satisfaction at her timing.

Fortunately, the dining table was circular, so there was no head of table as such, but Gina noted Gavin had taken the place formerly occupied by their father. Ann Taggart was on his right, Emily on his left. Gina handed round the cheesy toasts and took the vacant chair between Bill Taggart and Jack.

Bill never liked discussing business over a meal, and so

the talk was general – of holidays and sport, and the Taggarts' grandchildren. Jack noticed how well Gina played her part, flirting mildly with Bill, to his obvious pleasure, and chatting amiably to his wife. She combined that with effortless waitressing, clearing away quickly and efficiently before bringing in the main course. The roast lamb was cooked to perfection, accompanied by crisp roast potatoes, buttery-minted new potatoes and an assortment of fresh vegetables.

'That was delicious, my dear,' Bill beamed at her, patting his stomach as he finished his second helping.

'Yes, and such a treat,' Ann put in. 'My daughter-in-law's hopeless – if it can't be shoved into the microwave, she doesn't cook it! I fear for the children's health, really I do.'

'The young men in London must be blind or brain dead not to have snapped you up, Gina,' Bill said genially. 'Are you married, Jack?' he asked, with what Gina felt was a cringe-making non-change of subject.

'Perhaps she doesn't want to be snapped up,' Ann piped up before Jack could reply. 'Girls are more choosy these days, and quite right too. I bet you've had dozens of proposals, haven't you dear?'

'Well,' Gina laughed, aware of Jack's quizzical gaze on her, 'dozens of propositions certainly! Not quite the same thing at all. Now, pudding anyone? Emily, give me a hand with these, will you?' she asked, getting to her feet to clear away the dishes.

'I will,' Gavin offered quickly. Too quickly, Jack thought suspiciously and, with a smile of apology to Emily for leaving her alone with the guests, he silently followed the twins. He paused outside the kitchen doorway, out of sight but able to hear what was being said.

'...Told you he must have a personal reason for being

involved in the company,' Gavin was saying. 'It must be you!'

'How much have you had to drink?' Gina asked lightly, retrieving the desserts from the fridge, and piling a selection of cheeses onto a tray of fresh fruit. 'Carry this…'

'In a minute, ' Gavin interrupted. 'Don't you get it? It was Bill banging on about marriage that made me twig. Dad was always so insistent that the business remained a family concern. Well, the only way that can continue now is if you marry Jack Dawlish!'

'I'd rather marry Jack the Ripper!' Gina retorted, unable to take his theory seriously. Jack's brows rose at her comment – under different circumstances, it would constitute a challenge he couldn't resist. But…talk about getting hold of the wrong end of the stick! Peter Bruce would turn in his grave at the very thought of a marriage between him and Gina. He had heard enough and returned to the dining room but resolved to set Gina straight as soon as they were alone.

'Are you sure you've never met him before?' Gavin persisted, still holding the tray of cheese and fruit, and watching her put coffee on to percolate. 'Perhaps at one of those City lunches you and Sophie cater for?' he suggested, but Gina shook her head.

'I'd have remembered. No, I met him for the first time at the reading of the will. You're wrong, Gav,' she told him firmly. 'Just think about what you're saying – the idea's ludicrous! He doesn't even like me. Why on earth would he agree to marry a total stranger just to get his hands on a business which, according to you, is small by comparison with his other interests?'

'Mm, yes, you have a point,' Gavin said grudgingly. 'I still think he has a personal agenda though, something we know nothing about,' he muttered stubbornly. Gina raised her eyes heavenwards and pushed past him.

'You're crazy,' she said flatly, then plastered her hostess smile on her face before re-entering the dining room. She didn't for one second accept Gavin's explanation of Jack's intervention in their lives, but shot him a nervous grin as she sat down beside him. There was something about the smile he bestowed upon her in return that made her uneasy. It was...wolfish? No, not quite, more like the cat that had got the cream...or was anticipating having the cream...? She snatched up her wine glass and gulped down the contents, and pushed away her dish of syllabub, her appetite gone.

'Shall we have coffee in the drawing room?' she suggested when everyone had finished eating. Gavin poured brandy while Gina handed round coffee and offered a selection of the *petit fours*.

'Ooh, home-made, how lovely!' Ann bit into a peppermint cream and eyed the marzipan fruits wistfully, trying not to think about how many calories she had already consumed. 'I really mustn't eat any more though,' she declined regretfully.

'Take some with you, for your grandchildren,' Gina offered. She knew she would be tempted to make a pig of herself and eat them if no one else did. She fetched a container from the kitchen and, as she began piling the sweets inside, Jack came over to her.

'You're not giving them any coffee and walnut fudge, I hope?' he asked quietly, so as not to be overheard by the others.

'You've already eaten it all,' she retorted, then with an 'Oh!' she turned quickly to Ann. 'The children don't suffer from nut allergies, do they?'

'No,' Ann assured her.

'Great.' Gina smiled and continued with her task. 'It

wouldn't be good for business if I murdered the little angels, would it?' she murmured to Jack. She had her back to the Taggarts. Jack, unfortunately for him, did not, and struggled to keep his face impassive. How had her father resisted the temptation to wring her lovely little neck?

The party broke up shortly before midnight, and, after the front door had closed behind the guests, the others exchanged hopeful glances as they expelled breaths of relief.

'It seemed to go well,' Gavin said cautiously, crossing his fingers superstitiously. 'Bill's promised to introduce me to a couple of new prospects at the Trade Fair next week. He kept hinting about cost though, but I'm pretty sure he'll give us the contract if we shave, say…three per cent off the price.'

'Great,' Jack nodded. 'It would be worth it. Talking of contracts, how did you get on with the Carlisles?'

'Jerry Carlisle and his girlfriend are coming to spend the weekend with Emily and me,' Gavin told him. 'I'll show him around the factory and take them to the rugby club for dinner on Saturday evening.' His tone and slightly belligerent stance dared Jack to object to his plans, to insist on being present. Jack felt Gina's pleading gaze on him, silently begging him not to do just that, even though his instinct told him to.

'Jerry Carlisle?' he queried calmly. 'Doesn't Richard Carlisle run the company?'

'He's retiring – and handing over the reins to his son!' Gavin informed him tightly. Ouch! Gina winced.

'I see.' Jack was non-committal.

'Jerry and Gavin are old friends,' Gina put in quickly.

'Really?' Against his better judgement, Jack decided to give Gavin the chance to put the deal together, and hoped he wouldn't regret it. The Carlisle contract was the second most important after Taggart's. Uncomfortably aware that he was doing so to please Gina rather than Gavin, he smiled at the younger man. 'In that case, I'll leave it to you,' he said casually, then turned to Gina before Gavin could respond. 'It seems your culinary skills won't be required this weekend after all.'

'Oh, great. You mean I get the weekend off for good behaviour?' she grinned.

'You get the weekend off,' Jack said dryly.

'She's welcome to come along,' Gavin put in, deliberately emphasising the 'she'. Jack ignored him, but Emily's lips tightened in annoyance.

'That wouldn't be very tactful, darling,' she forced a smile as she slipped her arm through his. 'Jerry's bringing his girlfriend, after all.'

'Oh, right! Of course, Jerry's always had the hots for Gina!' Gavin laughed, his humour restored. His dark eyes rested on Jack maliciously. Despite Gina's scornful dismissal of his marriage theory, he was convinced Jack Dawlish had an ulterior motive. 'Perhaps it would be better if Jerry leaves what's-her-name at home and Gina joins us for the weekend. I'm sure she could persuade him to sign anything!'

'What am I – live bait?' Gina scowled at him. Besides, she had noticed Emily's less-than-enthusiastic reaction to Gavin's suggestion. What was her problem? she wondered. Whatever it was, she didn't want to get involved. 'I shall be going back to London for a couple of days,' she said firmly. 'Now, unless you want to help with the washing-up…'

'We're outta here,' Gavin said quickly, heading for the door. 'Goodnight, sis.'

'Goodnight.' Gina was smiling as she locked up behind them, then she walked wearily back into the drawing room and sank down on to the sofa. She kicked off her sandals with a sigh of relief and put her feet up on the coffee table, then removed her earrings and put them to one side.

'Brandy?' Jack asked, shrugging off his jacket and loosening his shirt and tie.

'Mm, yes please,' she yawned, resting her head back against the cushions. Her hair, still pinned atop her head, made the movement uncomfortable and, sitting up straight again, she began to slowly pull out the hairpins. Jack, watching her, found her action strangely erotic and continued watching as her hair gradually tumbled down around her face. Of course, he realised suddenly, it was as if she were preparing for bed...

'Here,' he placed her brandy in front of her, and sat beside her to drink his own.

'Thanks.' Gina leaned forwards, shaking out her hair, then reached for the glass and took a small sip. 'And thanks for not insisting on dealing with Jerry Carlisle yourself. I'm sure Gavin can manage.'

'I hope so,' Jack stared down at his glass. 'Is it true that Carlisle has "the hots" for you?' he asked. Gina laughed.

'He fancies his chances with anything in a skirt,' she replied.

'You're wearing trousers,' he pointed out, grinning.

'I guess that's me off the hook then,' she turned and smiled at him. Jack was dimly aware that they were both tired enough and relaxed enough to let the situation get out of hand. And, for some reason he couldn't and certainly didn't want to remember, that would be a mistake...

'Gina? We have to get one thing straight,' he said.

'Mm?'

'I overheard Gavin's theory about your father expecting

me to marry you,' he told her. 'Very imaginative, but simply not true.'

'Oh.' Gina blushed slightly, but the brandy stopped her from feeling really embarrassed. 'I told him he was wrong – not even Dad's Victorian attitudes stretched to arranged marriages.'

'You also told him you'd prefer to marry Jack The Ripper,' he reminded her, his grey eyes glinting.

'Oops! Sorry…' Gina smiled at him impishly. 'Serves you right for eavesdropping,' she added, stifling another yawn.

'I need to, to keep one step ahead of you and your brother,' Jack said ruefully. Their father had likened them to a pool of silver mercury, easily parted into two but immediately reforming into one entity, the division not even noticeable. He sighed and moved away from the temptation she offered, warm and sleepy-eyed.

'Were you serious about washing up tonight?'

'No,' she shook her head. 'I'm going to bed as soon as I can summon the energy to climb the stairs.'

'Do you need help with the buttons on that top?' Jack asked, his fingers itching to undo them, slowly, one-by-one, kissing each inch of creamy skin as it was revealed. But Gina shook her head, smiling.

'No, now my hair's loose, I can simply pull it over my head. I made the mistake earlier of doing my hair before I got dressed,' she explained, then said, 'do you always offer to undress the hostess of your dinner parties?'

'No, I usually say "thank you and goodnight" and put her in a taxi home.'

'Usually?'

'Always,' he amended.

'She's not…your girlfriend then?' Gina meant to sound casual, but was afraid she sounded anxious, jealous. Ever since she had told him she didn't give a toss if he had a million girlfriends, the question of who and how many had dominated her thoughts.

'No,' Jack shook his head. But that only told her that the woman who hosted parties for his London-based clients wasn't his girlfriend, she realised. It didn't mean he didn't actually have a girlfriend, just that, for some reason, she wasn't suitable to mix with his business colleagues. His girlfriend could be a dumb blonde, or…a lap dancer… A smile played around her lips and she eyed Jack from beneath her lashes.

'What's funny?' he asked lazily, reaching out and tracing her smile with one finger.

'I'm trying to imagine you with a lap dancer,' she said truthfully. His brows shot up.

'I'm not even going to try and make sense of that. One of us has had too much to drink – and I don't think it's me.' He stood up and reached for her hand to haul her to her feet. He gazed down at her for a long moment, fighting the desire to make love to her. 'You were terrific this evening. Thank you,' he said sincerely.

'Only following orders, sir!' Gina saluted, or tried to, but smacked herself in the eye instead. 'Ow!' The brandy had really gone to her head, she thought. Jack laughed at her. She aroused him, amused him, interested him as no woman had before. In short, she was dangerous. He grabbed her shoulders, spun her round until she was facing the door, then gave her a gentle shove.

'Bed,' he told her firmly. 'I'll clear these glasses away.'

'OK.' Gina headed for the stairs and hauled herself up. At the top, she looked back down and saw Jack passing through the hall to the kitchen. 'I think I do need help with these buttons,' she called down to him.

'Tough. Either tear them off or sleep in the damned

thing,' Jack ground out, his self-restraint at breaking point.

'OK.' Gina agreed amiably. A few seconds later, Jack jerked to a halt when he heard the unmistakable sound of ripped material. He stared resolutely down at the tray of glasses he was carrying. I will not look up. I will not look at her, he repeated, over and over.

When he went upstairs, her room was in darkness, the door closed. Refusing to admit his disappointment, he turned towards his own room. The gold top lay on the carpet outside his door. He groaned, but managed to ignore the invitation – if indeed that was what it was – and went, alone, to bed.

chapter seven

When Gina awoke, she had no memory of the last twenty minutes of the previous evening, other than that she had been alone with Jack. She clearly remembered the dinner party, the Taggarts' departure, then the rather tense conversation regarding the Carlisle contract, before Gavin and Emily had also left. After that, zilch. Only the vague feeling that she really ought to remember something…and where on earth was her top? she wondered, as she gathered up her laundry to take downstairs. Surely she…no, she'd have definitely recalled *that*!

A long, cool shower didn't help her amnesia, but she felt a strange reluctance to face Jack, so she ignored her need for strong coffee until she saw him leave. Only then did she venture downstairs.

'Breakfast?' Mary enquired cheerfully.

'Ugh,' Gina grimaced. 'Just coffee, then I'll start on this mess,' she said, gazing glumly round the kitchen, which seemed to have every available surface piled high with dirty crockery and leftover food. 'Did you enjoy your day off?'

'Yes, thank you. Would you like me to see to the dining room?'

'Yes please.' Gina gulped down coffee, then began stacking the dishwasher.

'Did the party go well?' Mary asked, re-entering the kitchen. She bundled the tablecloth and napkins into the washing machine and switched it on. The noise, coupled with that from the dishwasher, made Gina's head ache.

'Fine,' she said. 'Um, you haven't seen my gold top, have you? The one with buttons down the back?' The description triggered something in her brain, but the memory was so fleeting she couldn't make sense of it.

'It was in the laundry basket,' Mary told her.

'Really?' Gina's brow creased. 'I must have been drunk – it needs dry-cleaning.'

'That's what I thought, so I've put it with the other things,' Mary assured her. 'You can drop them off when you take Jasper to the vet.'

'Oh, no, I'd forgotten about that,' Gina said guiltily, and thoughts of Jasper drove the puzzle of her top from her mind. She checked the time, retrieved Jasper's travelling basket from the cellar and then went in search of him. He was asleep in one of his favourite sunny spots in the garden, but made no demur when she picked him up and cuddled him. However, his purring stopped abruptly when he spied the basket and he turned reproachful eyes on Gina.

'I know it looks like a budgie cage and is terribly undignified, but you have to go in it,' she told him firmly. She still had recurring nightmares about the one time she had taken pity on him and let him loose inside the car. He had somehow managed to squeeze beneath the pedals, making braking impossible unless she flattened him. Only by yanking on the handbrake and veering on to the pavement had she avoided both car crash and cat murder. Needless to say, the incident was a secret between her and Jasper. She had never dared tell her father or, even worse, Gavin, for he would never have let her hear the end of it.

Jasper yowled pitifully as soon as he was fastened into the basket, and the noise became even louder and more frequent once they were on their way. As a back-seat driver, he was more critical than her father and Gavin

combined, Gina thought, trying to close her ears to the
sound. Fortunately, the journey was a short one. Luckily,
too, the surgery wasn't full and she didn't have to protect
Jasper from the interest of an Alsatian dog for too long,
much to both her and Jasper's relief.

'Hello, Gina,' Steve Forrest's face lit up at the sight
of her.

'Hi,' she smiled, placing the basket on the examination
table and unfastening it. Jasper stalked out, his tail waving
in disapproval of his incarceration.

'Now then, Jasper, let's have a look at you.' Steve's
voice and hands were gentle as he examined the animal.
From his own records and the cat's age, he was expecting
to find worsening problems with arthritis and kidneys, but
he quickly suspected something more. Aware of Gina
watching anxiously, he kept his features impassive and
smiled reassuringly as he straightened.

'I'd like to keep him here and run some tests – he's
getting on a bit, aren't you, old boy?'

'Oh.' Gina stroked Jasper's head. 'Yes, OK,' she
agreed. 'When can I come and collect him?'

'I'll phone you tomorrow, when…'

'Tomorrow?' she looked at him in dismay. She didn't
think Jasper would appreciate being left here at all, never
mind overnight.

'Yes, the tests will take a while,' he said calmly.

'I don't think he'll settle,' she told him doubtfully.

'He'll be fine. Won't you?' Steve tickled Jasper and the
cat rubbed his head against Steve's hand affectionately.
Gina relaxed a little. She had often thought it was
amazing, how animals seemed to instinctively trust vets,
despite the horrors inflicted on them. After all, you
couldn't explain to them why they had to have injections
or whatever, but despite hating the car journey, all four

Bruce cats had been invariably docile once they were at the surgery.

'Well, if you think it's necessary…'

'It's better to be thorough,' Steve insisted.

'Yes,' she nodded, 'OK then.' Still she hovered, loath to leave him.

'Shoo!' Steve grinned at her. 'Don't worry, we'll take good care of him.'

'Yes,' she said again, stroked Jasper for a moment more, then turned to leave. She had a lump in her throat and tears stung her eyes as she got back into the car, and she chided herself for being so silly.

Back at the house, Mary greeted her with the news that Emily wanted to speak to her urgently.

'Oh, no, is Jack on the war-path?' she muttered, wondering what on earth she had done this time. However, she phoned the factory at once. Emily answered.

'It's me – what's up?' Gina asked.

'It's about those contract gardeners you hired. They're here and Harry's taken umbrage,' Emily told her, with some satisfaction Gina felt. 'Didn't you tell him what you'd arranged? He *is* the gardener, after all.'

'I forgot,' Gina admitted. 'The contract guys are only here for a one-off blitz – can't you explain that to Harry?'

'I'd rather you did,' Emily replied. 'The way he's grumbling and getting some of the other workers on his side, well, I wouldn't be surprised if they went out on strike. And I'd prefer not to have to explain that to Jack,' she added. You and me both, Gina thought.

'I'll be right there,' she sighed and hung up. 'I'm sorry, Mary, but I have to get to the factory,' she said apologetically, for the kitchen still looked as if a bomb had hit it. 'I'll be back as soon as I can.'

'Don't worry about it, it'll get done, sooner or later,' Mary said calmly. Gina smiled her thanks and dashed out to the car, praying Jack wouldn't hear about the furore she had caused. She should have explained to Harry, she realised that now, but it simply hadn't occurred to her. Perhaps Jack was right in his assessment of her – she *was* a liability to the company and didn't deserve a share in the profits simply because her name was Bruce.

When she pulled in to the car park, she immediately noticed the difference to the grounds in just a few short hours of concentrated work. The grass had been mowed, edges trimmed with razor-sharp precision, the flower-beds weeded and watered, and hedges and shrubs were being pruned into shape even as she watched. However, the speedy results were probably adding insult to Harry's injury, she realised, as she hurried inside.

'Where's Harry?' she asked Emily urgently.

'In the canteen, I think.'

'Jack still in the dark?'

'So far as I know,' Emily nodded. 'He hasn't come down from the office anyhow.'

'Great. If he does, stall him,' she instructed, and dashed off to the canteen. A group of drivers and packers were there, listening to Harry's grievance, as was Judy Finch, the rather militant sewing room supervisor, Gina noted with a sinking heart.

'...been here for more than twenty years,' Harry was grousing. 'I knew this place would go to the dogs once Mr Bruce went.'

'Harry, can I have a word please?' Gina asked sweetly, resisting the urge to remind them all that there was still a Mr Bruce. And a Miss Bruce, come to that. Well, maybe it was better to gloss over that bit – but Gavin knew what he was doing, even if she didn't. 'I am so sorry I didn't tell you about the gardeners coming today. It's a one-off, and no reflection on you,' she assured him. 'I'm sure you've seen the decorators here too – we're sprucing the place up before we invite buyers to come and look round,' she explained.

'I should have been consulted,' he grumbled.

'Yes, I know.' Gina kept her smile in face. 'Perhaps you could go and supervise them?' she suggested, hoping that wouldn't provoke yet another mutiny out in the grounds from the contractors. Harry seemed somewhat mollified by that and got to his feet.

'I suppose I'd better,' he agreed grudgingly, 'otherwise they'll make a total dog's breakfast of it that I'll be expected to sort out.' He sniffed, but then ambled off. Gina gave a sigh of relief. Too soon.

'What was that you said about buyers coming here?' Judy Finch demanded. 'I need to know if people are coming round my sewing room.'

'Yes, Judy, but I don't yet know exactly when they'll be coming,' Gina said calmly, resisting the impulse to ask, 'whose sewing room?' in the tone of voice she knew her father would have used. 'It certainly won't be next week because there's a big Trade Fair taking place, so it will probably be the week after. As soon as I have a definite date, I will certainly let you know,' she added, then suddenly inspiration struck. 'How would you feel about having some of the girls modelling the new lines?' she asked, hoping Jack or Gavin wouldn't complain about not being consulted first.

'Hm, well they'd probably be delighted – any excuse to get away from their machines for an hour or so,' Judy replied. Gina forbore to ask if Judy's own machine was in use at that moment.

'Why don't you think about it, which lines to model and

who would be the best models, and get back to me?' Gina suggested, with another falsely bright smile. God, she'd be qualified for a job at the United Nations if she kept this up!

'I'll do that,' Judy nodded, seemingly pleased. The drivers had drifted off in Harry's wake and now Judy also turned to get back to work. Gina closed her eyes and gave vent to a huge sigh of relief. Again, prematurely, as it turned out, for when she opened her eyes, she saw Jack leaning against the doorjamb, regarding her quizzically.

'Oh no! Who told you?' she demanded crossly. 'It wasn't necessary for you to come down here – it's sorted.'

'More by luck than judgement,' Jack said, and she bristled.

'I admit I made a mistake, but I retrieved the situation – OK?'

'A situation that should never have arisen,' Jack shot back, then relented, suggesting the fashion show had been a good idea, both in its own right and as a sop to the super-visor's hurt feelings. 'There's no harm done, this time. But just think things through properly in future and never underestimate how easily the workforce can take offence. And that always means trouble.'

'All right, you've made your point! I know you think my place is in the kitchen so, with your permission,' her voice dripped sarcasm, 'I'll go home and finish clearing up after last night.' She didn't wait for his agreement or otherwise, but stalked past him, head held high. Jack didn't try to stop her. Actually, she was right, well, partly. He was obviously becoming a male chauvinist pig in his old age, because after her exquisite cooking and seem-ingly effortless entertaining, he definitely did think her place was in the home. Not just the kitchen though – the bedroom featured highly in his imagination. His bedroom.

He shook his head to clear his thoughts and returned to his office. Good God, he'd soon be thinking of a nursery full of dark-haired, brown-eyed babies.

When Jack arrived back at the house late that afternoon – now spick and span and smelling of lavender furniture polish – he heard Gina's voice in the drawing room and paused on his way upstairs to unashamedly listen. She was evidently making plans for the weekend – with the blond beach bum? – and he quickly backtracked and entered the room.

'Hang on, Sophs, my parole officer's here,' Gina said into the handset. Jack relaxed. 'Sophs' must be Sophie Allinson. 'Why are you frowning?' Gina asked him. 'You said it was OK for me to go to London this weekend,' she reminded him.

'I know,' he nodded, 'and I wasn't frowning. I thought you might be making plans for tonight and we're going through this list of ex-clients – remember?' He opened his briefcase and took out the list of names Miss Pettit had handed him before he left the factory.

'I hadn't forgotten' she assured him, taking the list and scanning it briefly. She knew she had some ground to make up after the fiasco with the gardeners, so she asked politely, 'What time suits you? And do you want to eat before or after?'

'After,' he decided, and decided also to take her out to dinner. 'I'm going to take a shower then we'll make a start,' he said. Before he went upstairs, he located Mary and told her not to bother preparing a meal. Eat your heart out beach bum, he thought, as he ran lightly up the stairs. No date for you tonight!

Gina ended her call to Sophie and began studying the list of clients Jack wanted to try and win back. Most of the names were familiar to her; some she had known since childhood and had entertained many times in the past. However, there were some she had met only briefly, and she felt Gavin would have more success approaching them than either she or Jack. She made a mark against those she knew well and added further cryptic signs that had Jack frowning in perplexity when he joined her. He had showered and shaved, and was dressed in black trousers and soft wool grey sweater. He smelled faintly of soap and aftershave, and his black hair, still slightly damp from his shower, clung to his skull.

'What does "L" signify?' he queried.

'It stands for "lecher",' Gina told him. 'They'll love seeing the girls modelling bikinis – shove a contract under their noses while they're ogling them and they'll sign without even looking,' she promised, rather rashly.

'Very ethical,' Jack commented dryly. 'Did one of these guys get the trifle with cat hair?' he asked.

'Yes,' she nodded, then bit her lip in distress.

'What did I say?' Jack noticed her reaction.

'Nothing. I'm just worried about Jasper – I had to leave him with the vet for some tests,' she explained. 'I hate to think of him being there all night.'

'I know. You feel bad because you can't explain to him why you've apparently abandoned him,' he said. Gina looked at him in surprise at his understanding. She had half-expected him to scoff at her worries. Jack smiled slightly.

'I had a dog when I was a kid. I used to hate putting him in kennels when we went away on holiday. I always thought he must feel as if I'd put him in jail for a crime he hadn't committed,' he told her. Gina nodded.

'That's it exactly…oh, I know it's for the best and he'll be home tomorrow,' she said, and picked up the list again, forcing herself to concentrate. 'Gavin knows him well – and him,' she pointed out the names. 'It would probably be better if he spoke to them. I can phone the others. She frowned slightly, hoping they would all accept the invitation, but wondering if the house was big enough to accommodate them all. And would some of them feel slighted to know so many others had also been invited?

'Can you manage lunch here, if they all accept?'

'I was just thinking about that. The food's no problem – I can get a lot done next week and freeze it. It's just having enough room. We'll be OK if the weather stays fine…how about we do two lunches?' she glanced up at him. 'Give them a choice of which day to come? That will be easier to cater for and easier for you and Gavin to give them all the personal attention they'll no doubt expect. Let's face it, they're not stupid. They're shrewd businessmen and they'll know we're not inviting them simply for the pleasure of their company.'

'That's a good idea,' Jack nodded. 'Tell me what you know about them,' he added, settling back beside her on the sofa. The files were in his office, but he wanted this mood of working together to continue for as long as possible. 'The personal stuff – kids, hobbies, and so on.'

'Sure,' Gina agreed, feeling as comfortable as he did. In fact, she was almost disappointed when Gavin pulled up in his BMW and entered the house. His eyes narrowed when he saw Jack and Gina sitting so cosily together on the sofa, and he totally ignored Jack's less than warm greeting. Gina suppressed a sigh, wishing Gavin could find a way to work with Jack for both business and personal reasons.

'My mother-in-law is at my house. Again,' he grumbled to Gina. 'Do you want to come out for a meal?'

'Oh.' She didn't really want to, but bearing in mind his reaction to seeing her and Jack, she thought he'd sulk for days and be even less cooperative at the factory if she refused. She glanced at Jack. 'We've about finished, haven't we?'

'Sure,' he said neutrally, wishing too late that he had mentioned dinner earlier. But that would have placed her in an awkward situation, he thought. Gavin obviously resented her spending any time with 'the enemy'.

'I'll just go and change,' she told Gavin.

'Whatever for? You look OK as you are,' he said impatiently.

'I won't be a minute,' she promised.

'Just hold on a second,' Jack interrupted. 'While I've got you both here, I want to fix a time for an informal board meeting tomorrow.'

'I'm busy all day,' Gavin snapped.

'Then it will have to be at lunchtime, won't it?' Jack retorted. Gina bit her lip. Why couldn't they stop fighting? They were both at fault, she thought. Jack wasn't making allowances for Gavin's natural feeling of resentment and Gavin wasn't prepared to accept that Jack might just be saving the company from bankruptcy.

'Twelve o' clock?' she suggested brightly, darting a pleading look from one to the other.

'Oh, all right,' Gavin gave in with bad grace. 'I'll wait for you in the car,' he added to Gina.

'OK.' She turned and dashed upstairs, quickly changing into a simple shift dress of scarlet silk, and grabbing a jacket and bag before running downstairs again.

Jack watched moodily as the twins drove off, then wandered into the kitchen to make himself a sandwich.

'I'll do that for you.' Mary had heard him banging plates and cutlery and hurried in. Peter Bruce would never have dreamed of catering for himself, even on her days off, she'd had to leave meals already prepared for him.

'There's no need,' Jack smiled at her. 'I'm used to looking after myself. You and Gina have been spoiling me,' he added.

'I thought you were taking her out?'

'So did I,' Jack muttered, then he smiled again. 'She's gone out with Gavin.'

'Oh. It's nice that they're so close, isn't it?' Mary beamed. Wonderful, Jack thought bleakly. Out loud he said, 'Did you know their mother? Vivienne?'

'Only slightly. I didn't come to work here until after she died, poor lady,' Mary shook her head sadly, 'but she was a familiar figure in the town.'

'What was she like?' Jack asked curiously.

'Very pretty and vivacious, always had a smile and a word for everyone,' Mary said warmly. 'Of course, she was much younger than Mr Bruce and…' she hesitated, but they were both dead now so where was the harm in gossiping? Besides, Jack might be easier on the twins, Gavin particularly, if he knew more about the family.

'And?' Jack prompted, keen to hear an outsider's view of the Bruces' marriage. Peter Bruce had divulged very little and he knew, without asking, that the twins were biased in favour of their mother.

'Well, there were plenty of people who claimed she only married him for security and found her fun elsewhere, but I don't know if there's any truth in that. They did seem an unlikely couple though. He was never what you'd call friendly or approachable, even before Vivienne died. From what I saw of her, she was a wonderful mother. I'm sure she could have hired a nanny if she'd wanted to, but she always took care of them herself. She would play with them for hours down on the beach, or take them to the playground when they were little. And Gina told me once that she taught them both to read and write before they started school. She used to drive them there and pick them up every afternoon – they attended the local primary school. It was only after her death that their father sent them away,' she added, her mouth tightening with disapproval. 'I told him they'd be no trouble to me here. In fact, I only took the job because my heart went out to them, but he was adamant that they go away.'

'Hm.' Jack was non-committal. Peter Bruce had confided to him his reason for opting to send the twins to boarding school, but he didn't feel inclined to enlighten Mary. 'A difficult situation for a widower,' he said, then picked up his plate. 'Excuse me, Mary, I have some more work to get through,' he told her and headed back to the study.

'You and Dawlish looked very cosy,' Gavin was scowling into his beer. Gina sighed.

'Oh, not again! And can't you call him Jack? He's not a complete ogre, you know.'

'You've changed your tune,' Gavin eyed her suspiciously. 'Are you sure he's not hitting on you?' he asked. Gina tried not to squirm. She had a vague memory of her more or less 'hitting on' Jack the night before. And he had turned her down.

'I told you – you've got the wrong idea about him. He heard what you said about Dad planning to marry me off to him, and told me very firmly that it isn't true. I think he was amused by the very idea,' she finished.

'You sound as if you're sorry it's not true,' Gavin said sharply, unwilling to give up his theory so easily.

'Of course I'm not. But it's hardly flattering, is it? When

a man like Jack Dawlish thinks the prospect of marrying me is comical!'

'I guess not,' Gavin grinned. A pause, then the grin vanished and the scowl returned. 'What do you mean – a man like Jack Dawlish?' he asked. Gina hesitated.

'Well, he is rather attractive,' she said casually, in what was a gross understatement. Hastily, before Gavin could pursue this dangerous line of questioning, she changed the subject. 'How did Dad meet him?'

'The Chamber of Commerce invited him down to give an after-dinner speech to the members. I didn't go, but Dad did and apparently started chatting to him about the business. The next thing I know, Dad's showing him our accounts and asking for his help. Dad asked what I thought about Jack joining the board as financial director – not that he ever considered my opinion worth anything,' he said bitterly. 'I was against the idea, but then Dad died and, as you know, he left me with no choice but to accept the creep,' he finished.

'He must have had a good reason,' Gina said tentatively. Gavin snorted his derision.

'Apart from sheer bloody-mindedness?'

'Well, yes. His main concern was always the company – he must have thought we'd be better off with Jack…sorry,' she said hastily, aware of his pained expression. 'At least keep an open mind about Jack, and listen to what he has to say at tomorrow's board meeting before you jump down his throat,' she pleaded. 'I feel as if I'm caught in the middle.'

'I'll listen,' Gavin agreed grudgingly.

'Thank you. Now, we really have to decide about the house. There's tons of stuff to sort out before we can sell…'

'You do whatever you like,' Gavin shrugged, then he

brightened when he spotted one of his rugby teammates enter the bar. 'Mike! Over here,' he called and the man ambled over. 'You remember Gina, don't you?'

'Sure – how are you doing?' he smiled at her in friendly fashion. 'Can I get you both a drink?'

'Bitter for me and white wine for Gina,' Gavin told him, forestalling her refusal. Soon, more of Gavin's friends arrived and he cheered up considerably, she noted. She drank sparingly, for she still had a slight headache from the night before, and soon began to yawn in the over-warm, smoky atmosphere. Tiredness swept over her and she went to ask Gavin, now playing snooker, to take her home.

'After I've finished this game,' he barely glanced up.

'I'm tired,' she protested.

'I'll drop you off,' Mike offered, draining his glass. 'I'm leaving now and your house is on my route.'

'Thanks,' she smiled gratefully. 'See you tomorrow, Gav. And please don't wind Jack up by being late for the meeting.'

'Oh, OK. Stop nagging, I can get that at home,' he grumbled, lining up his next shot.

Mike's car was an open-topped sports model and the sea breeze gusting around her face during the drive home did much to banish both her headache and her tiredness.

'Would you like a coffee?' she asked out of politeness, when he pulled into the driveway.

'Yes, that would be great.' Mike climbed out of his car and followed her to the front door, when it was suddenly flung open and he found himself nose-to-nose with a grim-countenanced man of around his own age.

'Hi,' Gina greeted the guy casually. He ignored her and continued glaring at Mike, then looked pointedly towards the car. Mike got the message. Who was this guy – her husband?

'Forget the coffee, Gina,' he said hastily. 'I'll see you around. Nice meeting you,' he called caustically to Jack from the safety of his car. Jack's reply was to slam the door shut with the full force of his weight and anger. Just how many men does she have hanging around her? he wondered savagely, as he went after Gina.

'Well, you certainly went out dressed for the part,' he bit out. Gina glanced at him in surprise, then looked down at her simple chain-store dress in puzzlement.

'What do you mean?'

'A scarlet dress for a scarlet woman,' he gritted, acutely aware that the colour suited her creamy skin and dark hair, and that the silk cling to her luscious curves like a second skin. 'One gin and tonic and you're anybody's!' he finished contemptuously. Gina felt as shocked as if he had dowsed her in icy-cold water. She forced herself to stand her ground, albeit briefly, and a cool smile curved her mouth.

'I must protest – I never drink gin!' she drawled, then spun on her heel, desperate to get away from him before she succumbed to tears. Why had he become so hateful again? In such a short space of time, he had reverted to the despot of their first meeting. And she had just begged Gavin to listen to him, tried to convince him that Jack was no ogre…more fool she. She should have continued to listen to Gavin.

Jack watched her go, his fury was already beginning to abate and he acknowledged his emotion for what it really was – jealousy. Then he saw the almost imperceptible droop to her shoulders as she reached the kitchen and the rest of his unreasonable anger drained away. He ran after her and, grabbing her arm, pulled her round to face him.

'I'm sorry, I don't even know why I said that. I know it's not true,' he said earnestly.

'I don't care about your opinion of me,' Gina stormed, her eyes large and luminous with the tears she refused to shed. Refused, too, to admit that she did care what he thought of her. 'You merely parrot whatever Dad told you about me. And that's what hurts – that my own father thought I'm a slut.'

'He didn't think that,' Jack denied quickly.

'He obviously said something to give you that impression!'

'No,' he said again, cursing himself for the unwarranted insult. He already held one hand, now he reached for the other, and held them loosely, wanting to pull her into his arms but afraid of rejection. 'He worried about you living alone in London, nightclubbing…'

'So I go to a nightclub occasionally – big deal!' she interrupted hotly. 'That doesn't mean I take drugs or sleep around.'

'I know,' he soothed her, moving closer and slipping his arms around her waist. She resisted for a moment, then relaxed into his embrace.

'Did he…did he really worry about me?' she asked in a small voice.

'Yes.' Jack sensed there was another question, one she didn't dare ask, so he answered it anyway. 'He loved you, Gina,' he said quietly. 'I guess he didn't know how to show it other than by giving you money and freedom, even though he would have preferred to have you living here, where you'd be safe.'

Gina digested that in silence for a long time, resting her head against Jack's chest, comforted by the steady beat of his heart beneath her cheek and the strength of his arms around her.

'I accused him of killing my mother,' she whispered finally. Jack's arms tightened around her but he said nothing. He already knew that, and was becoming uncomfortably aware that he knew far more about the family than Gina could ever imagine. 'I kicked him at the funeral,' she continued, still in a whisper he had to strain to hear. 'I told him it was his fault, that I wished he had died instead of her…' She stopped speaking, and gave a sound that was half-hiccup and half-sob.

'I'm sure he understood your feelings,' Jack said gently. But Gina shook her head firmly in denial.

'No, I don't think he ever forgave me, not just for what I said, but because I said it, shouted it, in public. I…' she hesitated. 'I think that's why he sent us away to boarding school,' she told him, in a voice that quavered with long ago pain and loss. Jack closed his eyes in despair. He knew for sure that that hadn't been behind Peter Bruce's decision, but he couldn't tell her the truth, partly because he had promised not to, and partly because it would hurt her more than her present belief that boarding school had been a punishment.

'He forgave you – not that he ever thought you had done or said anything that required forgiveness,' he amended hastily. 'I know that he blamed himself for letting your mother drive off that night, so he could hardly be angry with you for thinking the same, could he?' he asked quietly. Gina didn't reply but relaxed against him even more and then gave vent to a huge sigh, as if a massive load had been lifted from her shoulders. But then she pulled back against his arms and looked up into his face.

'How do you know so much?' she asked slowly, a slight frown creasing her brow. Jack silently cursed his loose tongue. The trouble was, part of him wanted to tell her the whole story, wanted to be rid of the secret that was becoming daily, hourly, more of a burden than he could ever have imagined. It had been so easy to assure Peter

Bruce that he would look after the twins' financial interests without them ever discovering why he had been entrusted to do so. He hadn't for one second considered the possibility of becoming personally, emotionally, and oh so physically drawn, to Gina.

'Sometimes it's easier to confide in a stranger than in someone close,' he replied finally. After a moment, Gina nodded, seemingly accepting his explanation. But the acceptance brought her earlier grievance back to the forefront of her mind and she pushed roughly at Jack's chest until he let his arms drop to his sides. Now what? he wondered uneasily. Had he unwittingly given something away?

'Why did you accuse me of being a slut?' she demanded furiously.

'Ah.' Jack grimaced. 'I'm sorry, really I am. It's just that every time I turn round, you seem to have a different bloke hanging around you,' he said ruefully. 'You've spent very little time in Falworth during the past few years, yet you have half the male population panting at your heels.'

'Oh.' Gina regarded him thoughtfully, a slight smile tugging at the corners of her mouth. 'Your jealousy is flattering, but unnecessary,' she mocked him with the words he had used to her about Emily the previous day. Jack grinned in acknowledgement. 'I was tired and Gavin was involved in a game of snooker, so Mike offered to drive me home. That's all,' she explained.

'You invited him in for coffee,' Jack growled, and she laughed.

'So? I was only being polite. I knew you and Mary were here if he tried to pounce. Anyhow, he knows Gavin well – he wouldn't risk being thumped by him,' she added. Jack tried not to wince at the thought of being on the receiving end of the muscular rugby player's fist. Gavin already hated and resented him, and he wouldn't need much encouragement to try and inflict bodily harm.

'Does Gavin regularly thump men who, er, pounce?' he asked casually.

'Only if I ask him to! Do you want to put it to the test?' she asked, her eyes alight with mischief.

'Do you want me to pounce?' Jack countered, not totally convinced that after his crack about gin and tonic, she wouldn't actually enjoy seeing Gavin at his throat. Gina gave that her full consideration. The answer was 'yes' but she didn't quite dare say it.

'Forget I asked,' Jack said quickly, his conscience kicking in! If she knew the truth, she would be horrified, might well hate him as much as her brother already did, albeit for a different reason. And, of course, she would tell Gavin…and he couldn't risk telling her, not only because of his promise to her father, but because he had to make sure the company could survive without him at the helm. Only then could he allow himself to contemplate a relationship with Gina, one based on the truth. He could only pray that she would understand and not hold him accountable for what had happened so many years ago.

'Asked what?' she grinned, hiding her disappointment, and turned from him to go and fill the kettle. 'Coffee?'

'No, thanks. I should be getting back to work. Goodnight, Gina.'

'Goodnight,' she echoed. She heard his footsteps retreating, then spun round as she heard him re-enter the kitchen. Except it wasn't Jack – it was Mary. 'I'm making coffee – would you like a cup?'

'No thanks, poppet. I'm looking for my library book…oh, here it is,' Mary picked it up, then paused. 'Gina?'

'Yes?'

'I don't want to interfere…' She had come downstairs earlier in search of her book and had heard Jack's unprovoked attack on Gina's morals, and had guessed what lay behind it. 'I thought you might like to know that Jack wanted to take you out to dinner this evening. I think he was disappointed when you went off with Gavin.'

'Oh!' Gina felt swamped by sudden happiness and her smile lit up the room. 'Thanks for telling me.'

'You're welcome.' Feeling she had done the right thing, Mary went off to read in bed. Gina followed her upstairs soon after, and still had a smile on her face as she fell asleep.

chapter eight

Jack, in stark contrast to Gina, spent an extremely restless night tossing and turning, tormented by the seemingly unbridgeable gulf between what he wanted and what he could have. He was up at dawn and silently left the house to make his way down to the beach, washed clean after the tide.

It was deserted at such an early hour and he began to run, soon feeling energised by the exercise and the salt-laden crisp breeze from offshore. He slowed as he neared the town centre and the small marina, pausing to cast an eye over the boats, and wondered if he should hire one for the duration of his stay in Falworth. Gina had said she used to go sailing. Oh, stop it, he groaned to himself. He should be endeavouring to spend less time with her, not more. Besides, he had too much work to do, both here and in London. If he wasn't careful, his City-based clients would take umbrage at his continual absences and transfer their business elsewhere.

The house was still quiet when he returned. He helped himself to cereal and toast, and took a second cup of coffee upstairs with him to drink while he showered and shaved and dressed for the office. He set off for the factory soon after seven, knowing from past experience that he could get through a huge pile of work before interruptions began around nine.

When Gina went downstairs, she found a brief note from Jack on the kitchen table. It was hardly a *billet-doux* though. 'Board meeting. Twelve o' clock. Don't forget.'

She wondered if the reminder meant he didn't expect her to be at the factory before then and could have the morning to herself, but decided not to push her luck. She made sure she was there by nine, beating Gavin who was suffering from both a hangover and earache from Emily for not staying at home the night before to dine with her and her mother. Gina came in for an ear bashing too, an undeserved one at that, she thought resentfully, initially too taken aback to halt Emily's tirade.

'He's a married man now, Gina!' Emily said, anger giving her rare courage to stand up to her beautiful and elegant sister-in-law.

'So?'

'I accept that he has to be away a lot on business. But when he is here, you shouldn't encourage him to behave as if he's still single...'

'I do no such thing,' Gina protested. 'For God's sake, Emily, he's twenty-three – hardly eligible for pipe and slippers and sipping cocoa in front of the TV in the evening! Anyway, he only came to see me last night because he's sick of constantly falling over your mother whenever he *is* home! It's you who needs to grow up and realise you're married, not Gavin!' she snapped. Emily's brief spurt of courage deserted her and, bursting into tears, she fled to the cloakroom, leaving the reception desk unattended.

'Oh, for...' Gina bit back what she had been about to say and sighed, wondering if she ought to go after her and apologise. But for what? Gavin had done nothing wrong. Nor had she, for that matter, except to go out with him for a meal and a drink. Emily would really have something to complain about if and when Gavin asked a girl who wasn't his twin to spend the evening with him!

When the phone began to ring, she glanced round for

the office junior who covered for Emily's absences from the desk. She was nowhere in sight though and hoping she could remember how to transfer calls without disconnecting the caller, Gina answered it herself.

'Bruce Casuals, good morning. How can I help you?'

'Jack Dawlish please,' said a cool feminine voice.

'Who's calling?'

'Stella Lawson.'

'Just one moment, please.' Gina dialled Jack's office extension.

'Yes?'

'There's a phone call for you – Stella Lawson,' she said neutrally.

'Gina? What are you doing on the switchboard?'

'Answering the telephone,' she replied, and heard him sigh.

'Ask a dumb question,' he muttered. 'Where's Emily?'

'Sobbing in the cloakroom, I think,' Gina said, rather more cheerfully than she should have.

'I am not going to ask why,' he sighed again. 'Put Stella through, will you?'

'Yes, sir. At once, sir,' she said, and offered up a silent prayer that she wouldn't cut the woman off. Jack would never believe she hadn't done it on purpose...as if she cared if Stella Lawson phoned him a dozen times every day. Who on earth was Stella Lawson anyway? Oh, she was probably his health-freak PA, she realised, and put it out of her mind.

While she was sitting by the phone, she took the opportunity to phone Steve Forrest, to enquire about Jasper and ask when he could come home. However, the receptionist informed her that Steve was in surgery, dealing with an emergency admission, and would phone her as soon as he was free. Gina left the factory number and hung up.

By this time, Emily had returned red-eyed, and was standing over Gina, bristling with indignation at – presumably – having her chair annexed. Or still irritated because Gina was alive. Whatever. Gina left her to her sulkiness and went upstairs, pausing by Petty's desk.

'Petty? Jack's PA – is her name Stella Lawson?'

'No. Grant. Ms Anna Grant,' Petty grimaced at what she perceived to be the affectation of using 'Ms'.

'Who's Stella Lawson then?'

'No idea – is it important?'

'No,' Gina said moodily, and returned downstairs to make her way to the sewing room. She had learned her lesson and would consult with Judy Finch, the supervisor, before beginning her round of please-come-and-see-us-and-place-large-orders phone calls.

As Judy had predicted, the girls were keen to become temporary models. So many of them, in fact, that the only fair way to choose the half-dozen needed, was to put all their names in a hat and pick them out at random. Gina wondered if she would provoke a strike if she suggested only those size ten and under the age of twenty-five be considered eligible to enter. Then she decided she probably would and kept silent. Rather reluctantly though, because the younger, slimmer girls would show off the clothes to best advantage, particularly the beachwear. Cowardly, she figured she would hand the problem over to Jack and let him make the decision.

A couple of guys from packing had already offered to rig up a catwalk for the girls to strut their stuff to better effect, and Gina gave that the go-ahead.

'Are you going to model too?' one of the girls asked Gina. She laughed but shook her head.

'No, I shall be doing the catering back at the house,'

she explained. She and Judy looked over the clothes that would be new to the ex-buyers and decided which to focus on.

'And don't worry about the modelling,' Judy said in a low voice, 'I'll make sure the right names come out of the hat.'

'I'll pretend I don't know what you mean,' Gina replied. 'But thanks!'

Back upstairs, she began making phone calls, starting with people she knew well. A couple made excuses, but most seemed pleased to hear from her and accepted the invitation. Whether they just wanted a free lunch and a chance to ogle bikini-clad girls was debatable, of course, but she would have done her part if she got them to Falworth and fed them. The rest was Gavin and Jack's responsibility.

Shortly before noon, she made her way to the board-room, arriving only seconds before Jack. There was no sign of Gavin and her heart sank. She had hoped she had convinced him to be less hostile, at least until he had heard what Jack had to say. To try and distract Jack from noticing Gavin was late, she told him of her morning's activities and he nodded his approval.

'I'm not too happy about the makeshift catwalk though,' he frowned. 'If one of the girls falls off or, worse, falls through it, we would be liable under the Health and Safety at Work Act.'

'You could try it out first,' she suggested. 'If it holds your weight, it will certainly hold theirs!'

'Ooh, thanks,' he put a hand on his hip and minced in camp fashion around the room. Gina giggled.

'It suits you,' she told him.

'What the…?' Gavin had paused in the doorway.

'Watch it, Gav – it's not me Dad wanted him to marry

– it's you!' she told him and laughed even more at the expression on both men's faces.

'OK, let's get down to business,' Jack tried to restore order. They all sat down and he passed each a slim folder. 'I don't want to go into details today, but please read the proposals outlined in here and we'll discuss them all fully at the next board meeting. Feel free to take independent advice if you wish…'

'We will,' Gavin interrupted. Gina, sitting opposite, aimed a kick at him under the table. He had promised he would at least listen!

'What I do want to discuss today,' Jack continued as if Gavin hadn't spoken, 'is the long-term management structure. I suggest Miss Pettit become the office manager in charge of administration, and be appointed to the board in due course,' he said. The twins exchanged a look. Petty was on their side…

'Would she get any shares?' Gavin asked.

'Yes. Out of my fifty-five per cent,' he clarified quickly before Gavin could speak. 'We also need to take on a financial director…'

'I thought that was your job,' Gavin interrupted again, his tone truculent. Gina stretched out her foot once more, harder this time.

'It is for now, but my business interests are in London. Gina, that's my ankle you keep kicking, not Gavin's,' he said mildly.

'Oh. Sorry!' she collapsed into giggles. Jack shook his head in despair but smiled at her. Even Gavin gave a reluctant grin and the tension in the room eased somewhat.

'As I was about to say,' Jack went on, ' you need a permanent financial director to run things here, Gavin. You don't have a degree in either business studies or economics. I want to get on to a recruitment agency immediately.' He passed each a copy of the details outlining the position offered. 'The sooner we can get on with interviewing applicants the better.'

'You haven't mentioned a salary,' Gavin pointed out. 'Can we afford to pay the sort of money these guys would want?'

'I think the prospect of profit-sharing and a future seat on the board, together with a percentage of shares, will outweigh a probable drop in salary,' Jack explained. 'Also, living here might well appeal to someone with a couple of small children, someone who would prefer not to raise a family in London. And the difference in property prices will be an added bonus for him.'

'Or her,' Gina put in.'

'Or her,' Jack acknowledged with a slight smile.

'Do I get a say in who's offered the job?' Gavin demanded. 'I'm going to be working with him, after all. I'm not going to stand for you putting one of your lackeys in here to spy on me and report my every move to you!'

'Of course you'll be present at all the interviews,' Jack said calmly, determined not to lose his temper. 'Don't worry, Gavin, I've no desire to spend any more time in Falworth than is strictly necessary.'

'That's the best news…'

'Gavin! Shut up,' Gina said crossly. Surely he could see that, by giving shares to Petty and the new guy, Jack would in the future no longer have a majority shareholding? Even she had worked that out! The twins glared at each other and Jack wisely didn't intervene. He frowned though when the phone rang, and snatched it up.

'Yes? What? Oh, very well,' he sighed, resisting the urge to tell Emily to disconnect the caller, and held out the receiver to Gina. 'For you. Steve Forrest.'

'Oh,' she took the phone, feeling suddenly apprehensive. 'Steve?' She listened for a while and the two men watched her, but for different reasons.

'Oh no!' She closed her eyes and bit her lip, as if trying not to cry. Jack thought. He glanced questioningly at Gavin.

'The vet,' Gavin explained tersely. 'What's up?' he asked urgently. Gina took a deep breath and blinked back tears.

'Steve says…Jasper's got cancer,' she stammered, her voice and lower lip trembling.' And, considering his age, he thinks we…we,' she swallowed, 'should have him…put to sleep.'

'Oh God.' Gavin snatched the phone from her hand to speak to Steve himself. Jack regarded Gina sympathetically, but guessed a hug or consoling words would result in the tears she was obviously desperately trying not to shed, so he made no move towards her.

'Tell him I'm coming to fetch him,' she told Gavin. 'He's not to…to do it at the surgery. Ask him to come to the house later,' she said urgently.

'OK,' Gavin nodded and relayed her message, then looked up. 'He'll do that,' he confirmed.

'Right.' Gina got to her feet, picked up the folder in front of her and looked around for her bag containing her car keys.

'Poor old boy,' Gavin said miserably after he had hung up. 'I feel awful. I should have noticed something was wrong – I see him more often than you do.'

'That's probably why you didn't realise,' Gina sought to comfort him. 'We all thought he was only suffering from old age…where on earth is my bag?' she demanded.

'I'll drive you over there,' Gavin told her, shooting a look at Jack which dared him to object. Jack had been about to make the same offer, but realised this was something the twins needed to do together.

'I'll find your bag and get someone to drive the Volvo back to the house,' he said instead.

'Thanks,' Gina nodded, forcing a wan smile, then she and Gavin hurried from the room.

Jack crossed over to the window and watched until they emerged outside. Gavin had a comforting arm around her shoulders and was talking to her as they walked. Gina nodded agreement to whatever he had said and climbed into the passenger seat, dabbing furtively at her eyes.

When Jack returned to 'The Beeches' at teatime, the twins were out in the garden with Jasper, so a red-eyed Mary told him. She would miss the cat as much, if not more, than anyone. Jack glanced out of the kitchen window and saw they were sitting on the lawn, Jasper curled peacefully on Gina's lap.

'I'll get that,' he told Mary when the front door bell pealed. He pulled open the door and scowled at the sight of the blond beach bum standing there.

'What do you want?' he snapped. Steve Forrest's brows rose in astonishment.

'I'm Steve Forrest, the vet. Gina is expecting me,' he said.

'Oh.' Belatedly, Jack noticed the medical bag the man was carrying and pulled the door wider to allow him entrance. 'They're in the garden,' he said. As he led the way, he suddenly realised what Gina had meant by her parting shot to him on the beach. She hadn't been arranging a date, well not for herself anyway. Gina looked on the brink of tears when she saw Steve enter the garden and approach.

'Are you sure?' her voice quavered. 'He seems happy…'

'I'm sorry, Gina,' Steve said gently. He knelt on the lawn beside them and opened his bag. Jack didn't like to intrude, but was heartily glad when Gavin spoke up.

'You don't need to be here,' he said gruffly. 'Go inside.'

'No, he's my cat too,' Gina insisted stubbornly. 'I'm staying.' She tried not to watch Steve as he clipped away a small piece of fur and removed a syringe from his bag. She continued stroking Jasper, murmuring to him and looking into his eyes. She didn't need Steve's softly spoken 'That's it' to know that Jasper was dead. All the light had gone from his eyes, although he still seemed to stare up at her. Her vision blurred as she carried on stroking the soft, warm fur, not noticing Steve's departure, nor Gavin going to fetch a spade from the garden shed.

'We'll bury him with the others,' he said and she allowed him to take the lifeless form from her and followed him to the bottom of the garden where Jasper's brother and sisters were buried beneath a cherry tree. All four cats had loved the tree, chasing the falling blossom in spring as if trying to catch confetti, and lying in its shade in summer.

Jack showed Steve to the door, then returned to watch the twins from the kitchen window. Gina suddenly stood up and ran back inside the house, but ignored Jack and Mary. Instead, she grabbed up Jasper's blanket and badly chewed rubber mouse, then dashed back to join Gavin. Jack moved away from the window only when the phone rang and then, feeling a strong reluctance to disturb the twins even though the burial was complete, walked out to speak to Gavin.

'Emily's just phoned – Jerry Carlisle has arrived,' he told him.

'Oh, no. Trust him to be early,' Gavin grumbled. He too looked suspiciously red-eyed, Jack noted, as he got to his feet. 'Will you be OK?' he touched Gina gently on the shoulder. She looked up and managed to smile.

'Yes, you go,' she urged him. She remained where she was though, kneeling beside the mound of freshly dug earth and, after a moment, Jack hunkered down beside her and silently offered her his handkerchief.

'Thank you,' she sniffed and dabbed at her eyes. 'I suppose you think I'm being childish?'

'Not at all,' he denied swiftly, and truthfully. 'I remember how bad I felt when my dog had to be put down. I cried for a fortnight,' he admitted. Gina looked up.

'How old were you?'

'Twelve,' he said. 'For months afterwards, I half-expected to see him come running to meet me when I got home from school, and was gutted all over again when realisation hit.'

'I know,' she nodded. 'I was upset when the other cats died, but this is worse somehow. Maybe because we made the decision to…to kill him, or maybe because he's the last one…' She fell silent for a moment then continued, 'We got them for our fourth birthday. We were only supposed to have one kitten each, but when we saw all four of them, we couldn't decide which we liked best, so Mum said we could bring them all home. It had to be a secret from Dad though. Luckily, they all had similar colouring so he thought he kept tripping over the same two!' she grinned suddenly at the memory.

'He knew there were four,' Jack said quietly.

'Oh, sure, he twigged eventually. But they had all settled in by that time and even he wasn't heartless enough to make us get rid of two of them.'

'You're wrong, Gina. He knew there were four the day after you brought them home. He went into the kitchen and saw them all asleep in their basket.'

'He told you that?' Gina stared at him puzzled. 'Why did he keep up the pretence of believing there were only two? He even said something along the lines of how amazing it was that two small kittens could be everywhere at once,' she remembered. She, Gavin and their mother had laughed over that.

'How could he say anything?' Jack countered. 'Your mother had given permission for you to have all four, despite knowing he had insisted on only two. I guess he saved face by pretending not to know. He always had to be the bad guy, didn't he Gina? The disciplinarian?'

'He liked it that way,' she shrugged.

'Did he?' Jack asked quietly. She stared at him for a long moment, then scrambled to her feet.

'It hardly matters now, does it?'

She went upstairs to her room and sobbed for a while. For Jasper, who had so often curled up on her bed on winter nights, for her father too perhaps, she realised, with a sense of shock that abruptly dried her tears. Had he felt forced into the role of disciplinarian, as Jack claimed? Felt compelled to be strict because their mother had never rebuked them, had laughed off their misdemeanours? No…she remembered all too well how the fun had always stopped the minute he had arrived home. Vivienne anxiously telling the twins to be quiet now, to go to the playroom because their father was tired and didn't want to be bothered by their noisy games.

'Who is it?' she called when a light rap sounded on her door.

'Jack. Are you OK?'

'Fine. Come in,' she said, wiping her eyes and going over to the mirror to check the damage her tears had wrought upon her face. Oh God, she looked awful! 'No!

Don't come in,' she panicked. Jack paused with his hand on the doorknob.

'Do you want to drive back to London with me?' he asked. 'I'm leaving shortly.'

'It's OK, I've got the Volvo…haven't I?' she asked, suddenly remembering she had left it at the factory.

'Yes, it's parked outside. But you're not used to driving it in London, are you? And you're upset – drive back with me,' he urged.

'But the traffic will be awful…'

'So? I only live about half-a-mile from you, so it won't make much difference to my journey time,' he told her.

'Really? Where do you live?'

'Just off Sloane Square…Gina, do I have to talk to the door?'

'Yes, I look dreadful,' she said candidly. And her make-up was in the bathroom, which she couldn't get to without him seeing her. 'Give me five minutes to freshen up, then a lift would be great. Thanks,' she accepted his offer. She didn't mind driving the bigger car in London, but parking it might well prove impossible.

'Right. I'll wait for you downstairs.' Gina waited for a moment to be sure he wouldn't catch a glimpse of her puffy, reddened eyes and blotchy cheeks, then dashed across the landing.

She bathed her face in cold water, pressing the flannel over her eyes until most of the heat had left them, then applied make-up to cover the remaining damage. She didn't need to pack much, since she had almost everything she would need in her flat, so she joined him downstairs within the promised five minutes.

In her overnight bag, however, was tucked the folder containing Jack's proposals for the company. Sophie's father, Dan Allinson, had offered his help when he had learned of Peter Bruce's death and, as a wealthy businessman himself, she hoped he would read Jack's proposals and give an unbiased opinion. The only other person she could think to ask was the company's accountant and, as Jack held fifty-five per cent of the shares, she wasn't sure how unbiased he might be.

'Ready to go?' Jack asked casually, purposely not looking directly at her.

'Yes.' She said goodbye to Mary, then followed Jack out to the car. 'God, what a dreadful day,' she sighed, as she leaned back in the passenger seat and closed her sore eyes against the glare of the sun.

'I know. You just have to keep telling yourself you did him a favour. The vet wouldn't have suggested it if he didn't think Jasper was in pain,' he said gently.

'Yes, I know,' she sighed again, then tried to put it from her mind. 'What plans do you have for the weekend?' she asked. Jack smiled slightly.

'Catching up on work, I'm afraid.'

'All weekend?'

'I expect so. You?'

'Um.' It seemed tactless to mention shopping, clubbing or anything remotely pleasurable or lazy if he were to be working. 'I'm not sure, just catching up with friends, finding out all the gossip I've missed,' she said vaguely.

'Gina, you've been away less than a week,' he pointed out dryly. 'How much gossip can you possibly have missed?'

'I know,' she grinned. 'It just seems longer than a week.' She stole a glance at him. A week ago, she had hated him...

'You're a city girl through and through, are you?' he asked lightly.

'I've enjoyed living in London for the past few years, but I'm not sure I want to stay forever.'

'Me neither. Strange, isn't it? We can't wait to head for the bright lights yet, after a while, we start longing for space and fresh air and no near neighbours. I sound ancient, don't I?' he suddenly realised.

'A bit,' she smiled at him. 'No, actually, you sound tired. It's just as well you've let Gavin and Emily deal with Jerry Carlisle this weekend.'

'Mm, I'm a bit uneasy about that...not Gavin,' he assured her quickly before she could leap – yet again – to her brother's defence. 'Not unless he and Carlisle get too drunk to discuss business,' he amended. 'No, it's Emily – she didn't exactly contribute much at the dinner party, did she?'

'I suppose not, but she's only met the Taggarts once before, I think. She knows Jerry quite well, and his girl-friend will be around her own age, so I think she'll be more at ease.'

'I hope so. Of course, you won't be there which will help,' Jack continued unthinkingly.

'What?' Gina sat up straighter and glared at him. 'What on earth does that crack mean?' she demanded.

'It was a compliment to you, believe it or not,' he told her, hiding a grin at her outraged expression.

'Not,' she informed him tersely.

'Truly, it was,' he assured her. 'Emily's intimidated by you, so I'm hoping she'll be more relaxed as a hostess if you're not there to watch.'

'Intimidated by me? Whatever for?' Gina asked in amazement.

'Beats me,' Jack shrugged. 'After all, you're not pretty, you can't cook, you're tongue-tied and awkward with guests...need I go on?'

'You told Emily she looked pretty.' Gina sounded more accusing than she had meant to. Sounded jealous actually, she thought, cringing.

'She did look pretty. But I was only trying to bolster her confidence. Before the Taggarts even arrived, she was feeling overshadowed by you and obviously low in self-esteem.' He paused. 'She'll have to learn how to cope better with social occasions, after all, you can't act as Gavin's hostess for ever.'

'Why not? I did it for Dad, I don't mind doing it for Gavin.'

'Emily would mind,' he said quietly.

'Well, she's got two choices then, hasn't she?' Gina snapped. 'She can either cultivate some social skills or let me do it.'

'OK, let's not fight about it.' Jack wished he had kept silent.

'You started it,' she muttered rebelliously.

'Yes, I did, and now I'm finishing it. End of discussion. OK?'

'Fine.' Gina folded her arms and stared resolutely out of the side window, her face averted from his. Jack drove in silence for a while, wondering how the conversation had degenerated into a near quarrel. But he guessed she was more upset about Jasper than anything he had said about Emily. He was right. Gina didn't want to think about what had happened to her pet, so ended the silence to distract her.

'Tell me about your dog,' she said suddenly. 'And the farm.'

'Very well.' Feeling on safe ground, he began to talk about growing up in a small farming community, and could feel the tension begin to leave her body.

'You mentioned once before that it's your mother's

farm – will she expect you to go back and run it one day?'

'No, it's not the life for me,' he said decisively. 'I think I also told you that she rents out the land? I guess she'll sell up altogether when she tires of running the house as a Bed and Breakfast. She only does that in the summer months anyway. She and a friend take long cruises to escape the British winter.'

'Do you have any brothers or sisters?'

'No.'

'What about your father? You said he lives abroad,' she remembered.

'Mm. Australia, as far as I know.'

'You don't keep in regular contact?'

'No.'

'Would it be rude to ask why?'

'Would it stop you if I said "yes"?' He turned to smile at her. 'Let's just say we don't see eye-to-eye on a lot of subjects. All subjects,' he amended.

'Oh.' Gina guessed he had probably taken his mother's side in the divorce, but a sideways glance at his rather grim expression stilled further questions.

The traffic congestion had eased somewhat by the time they reached central London, but the road outside Gina's apartment block was clogged with parked cars. However, Jack risked being clamped by blocking an exit and turned off the engine. Gina turned to him in surprise.

'Your flat's been empty all week – I'll feel better if I come in with you and make sure you haven't been burgled or acquired squatters,' he explained.

'Oh, thanks.' She didn't think it was necessary but appreciated the gesture. She grabbed her overnight bag from the car and hurried up the steps, unlocking the main entrance door, then the door to her own flat. Everything was as she had left it.

'Right, I'll be on my way. Enjoy your weekend. I'll pick you up on Sunday evening – about six?' he suggested. She nodded.

'That will be fine. Thanks for the lift. And don't work too hard,' she called after him. He waved in acknowledgement, but didn't reply. He dreaded to think of the pile of work awaiting him.

chapter nine

The flat seemed rather stuffy and airless, so Gina went through opening windows before going to shower and change. Then, rifling absently through her post, she phoned Sophie. It was Dan Allinson who picked up the phone.

'Oh, hello, Gina. No, I'm sorry, she's already left. Hang on…' his voice became distant as he spoke to his younger daughter to see if she knew where Sophie could be found. 'Is that a person or a place?' she heard him ask then, 'Gina? Apparently she's gone to Cleo's.'

'I know it. I might join her later. Actually,' she hesitated, 'would you mind if I ask your advice? About Bruce Casuals,' she added hastily, lest he thought he was about to be cast in the role of agony uncle.

'Of course I don't mind,' he assured her promptly. 'What can I do to help?'

'Well, my father left someone else in charge of the company over Gavin's head, and he's presented us with a list of proposed changes which he says are necessary to make the firm profitable again. According to him, we were heading for bankruptcy,' she said candidly, figuring there was no point in asking for advice if she didn't tell him the whole story. 'I wondered if you would look them over and see if you think he's acting in the company's best interests.'

'I'll have a look, certainly, but what makes you think he'd do otherwise?'

'I'm not sure. But Gavin doesn't trust him.'

'Ah. What's this man's name? I'll check up on him,' Dan Allinson assured her.

'Jack Dawlish.'

'I've heard of him, never met him though,' Dan mused. 'I'll make a couple of phone calls and see what I can find out. Do you want to drop those proposals over here? And a copy of the latest accounts would help give me the broader picture.'

'I don't have those, sorry.'

'Never mind. I'll go through the proposals first and make sure Dawlish hasn't any skeletons in the closet. Can you come over now?' He hadn't amassed a fortune by letting the grass grow under his feet!

'Yes, if you're sure it's convenient. Thank you; I'll be there as quickly as I can.' She had disconnected before remembering she had no car and would have to get a taxi. She decided it would be quicker to find one on the Kings Road rather than phone and wait for one to come to the flat.

She snatched up the folder, her bag and her mobile, then added her rape alarm to her bag. She hadn't felt the need to carry it in Falworth but, even though the evening was still light and sunny, she wouldn't venture out alone without it in London. She normally never gave it a second thought; it was part of the life of a young woman in a big city, but this evening its necessity depressed her. Perhaps Jack was right – the bright lights did pale after a while and one thought nostalgically of the more peaceful surroundings of one's childhood.

She hailed a taxi easily enough and gave directions to the Allinsons' large house in Belgravia. Sophie's sister, Loulou, opened the door to her and smiled. She was blonde and blue-eyed like Sophie but, as Sophie cheerfully admitted, she had the brains of the family. She was at university studying economics, and had already warned her father she would be after his company one day soon. For now though, she had been roped in by Sophie to cover for Gina's absence and was glad to see her back in London. For good, she hoped.

'Dad's expecting you – he's in the library,' she pointed towards the half-open door. 'Can I get you coffee, or a glass of wine?'

'No, thanks,' Gina declined the offer and walked over to the library, rapping lightly on the panelled door.

'Yes? Ah. Gina, come in,' he got to his feet gallantly and placed a chair beside his own for her to sit down. He got straight to the point. 'Jack Dawlish. He's well thought of. No one had a bad word to say about him, no buried bodies as far as I could ascertain,' he laughed. 'Why exactly does your brother distrust him? Or, forgive my frankness, my dear, is Gavin merely piqued because your father placed Dawlish in charge?'

'Well,' Gina hesitated, 'Gavin's upset about that, of course he is, especially when it has always been understood that he would inherit the majority shareholding. But he's convinced Jack has a personal reason for being involved because Bruce Casuals is such a small company compared to his other interests.'

'Hm. Gavin's what – twenty-three?' He raised an eyebrow and she nodded. 'He's very young for such responsibility. But that's something time and experience will easily take care of,' he smiled. 'It's when you're too old for things you need to start worrying!'

'I suppose so,' Gina returned his smile.

'Let me have a look at Dawlish's rescue package,' he nodded towards the folder and Gina passed it across to him. Dan read each page quickly but carefully, his features impassive until he reached the proposals regarding the two new appointments to the board. His brows rose and he peered at Gina over his spectacles.

'According to this, Dawlish is setting up a new management structure to support Gavin, and handing over part of his own shares. And he hasn't included himself in any future profit-sharing.'

'That's right,' Gina nodded. Dan frowned slightly.

'He obviously isn't in it for financial gain. Is there a family connection?'

'No. He only met my father a few months ago, or so Gavin said. Dad asked him to join the board but he died before that could be finalised.'

'Hm. Dawlish is either extremely altruistic, or Gavin is correct in thinking he has a personal motive. On the face of it, he has nothing to gain. But he has a sound reputation in the City and these proposals seem a positive move towards bigger turnover and higher profits. I don't think you need worry, Gina. A man like Dawlish wouldn't risk damaging his professional standing,' he said decisively, then a roguish smile curved his mouth. 'As for a personal reason –well maybe you need look no further than your mirror!'

'That's what Gavin said,' Gina felt herself blush. 'But I only met Jack a week ago.'

'Perhaps he's seen you around, at those lunches you and Sophie cater for, for instance?' he suggested.

'Gavin said that too,' she said slowly. Could it possibly be true? Yet he had derided the notion… 'Thank you for your time,' she stood up and he handed her the folder.

'You're welcome. If you'd like me to check over the accounts, I will do so gladly. Ask the company's accountant for a copy and send it to me.'

'Thank you.' They shook hands, in deference to it being a business meeting Gina supposed, since they hadn't done so since their first meeting some years before. Dan escorted her out and, upon learning that she had no car, insisted on seeing her safely into a taxi.

'Where to, luv?' the driver asked. Gina hesitated, then decided against joining her friends and gave him her home address instead.

Once inside the flat, she switched on some music and re-read Jack's future plans for Bruce Casuals. It had been easy to dismiss Gavin's insistence on what he called Jack's 'personal agenda', but now Dan Allinson agreed. Jack wasn't gaining anything from his inheritance other than a lot of hard work and even more grief from Gavin. She supposed there would be nothing to prevent him from taking a share of the profits at some point in the future but, according to Gavin, the money would be small change to him...

So, back to a personal reason. Her? Or Emily? It was possible – just – that he had seen her around London, or fallen for Emily when he was in Falworth, but there would have been a hundred easier ways of pursuing either girl if that was his aim. To have chosen instead to gain her father's trust – not easy! – and persuade him to leave him in control of the company – an action which had made both girls resent him...no, it was absurd.

This was something between Jack and her father, she realised suddenly, and a huge clue had been staring her and Gavin in the face all the time. Namely, that Jack had been invited to stay at 'The Beeches'. Their father had valued his solitude – even Mary had been expected to keep to her own suite of rooms when he was at home. Gavin had moved out years ago to a flat on the sea front and, until his marriage, she had stayed with him when in Falworth, not with her father. It was only after Gavin married Emily that she had occasionally stayed in her old room at 'The Beeches' to give the newly-weds their privacy. Yet Jack Dawlish had been welcomed by Peter Bruce, been given the run of the place...

She reached for the phone directory, determined to talk to Jack. She found the number easily enough. There were only two J.A. Dawlish's listed, and only one in the vicinity of Sloane Square. She began dialling, then paused, realising she needed to speak to him face-to-face. She restarted dialling, intending to ask if she could call on him, the paused again. Going in the evening could give the wrong impression, seem provocative...but she had to do something, otherwise she would puzzle over it all night. Determinedly she dialled again, the entire number this time. After all this dithering, he would probably have gone out or switched on the answer phone if he wanted to concentrate on his work, she thought ruefully.

'Yes?' He sounded distracted, tired, and Gina grimaced slightly.

'It's me, Gina,' she said tentatively.

'Hello there.' His voice was warmer now, she thought.

'I'm sorry to disturb you, I know you're very busy this weekend,' she said quickly, 'but I wondered if I could come and see you tomorrow? About your plans for the company,' she continued, which was only a white lie. 'I've asked someone to look at them for me...'

'I see. You didn't waste any time, did you?' he sounded quite unconcerned. 'Sure. What time? I'll be here all day.'

'About ten? In the morning, I mean,' she added hastily and heard a soft chuckle.

'Pity. Yes, ten will be fine.'

'Thank you. Goodnight.'

'Goodnight, Gina.' The words were a soft caress that lingered in her memory. But she needed some straight answers from Jack before...before what exactly, she didn't know. All she did know was that he had to tell her the truth about his involvement in her family's company.

She spent the rest of the evening dealing with the week's post, then checked her emails and replied to them before switching off her computer. Thoughts of Jasper were never far away though, and so she did what she usually did when she felt out of sorts and decided to cook.

Her kitchen, always tiny, seemed even more annoyingly so after the spacious room at 'The Beeches', but she set to anyway and decided to take a meal to Jack when she called on him the next day. She closed her mind to what Gavin would have said if he knew what she was doing, and gathered together ingredients for a sponge cake, sure that Jack would enjoy it and equally sure that it was something he probably only ate on his admittedly rare visits home. She already had a range of meat dishes in her small freezer and pondered which to take. She recalled his love of home-cooking, his enjoyment of Mary's chicken casserole and her own roast lamb. So she ignored the more exotic dishes and took out a steak-and-kidney pie to defrost, which he would only have to re-heat. If she didn't like the answers he gave to the questions she asked, well, she would give the food to the first homeless person she saw on her return journey home. Or shove the cake in his face!

She was stifling yawns by the time she had finished decorating the cake with a fudge topping, exhausted by the traumatic day, and went to bed. It was quite some time before she fell asleep though. She was unusually aware of the traffic noise and realised she had quickly become accustomed to the cries of gulls in Falworth and the distant sounds of waves breaking on the shore.

She was awakened by the ringing of her bedside phone shortly before nine. It was Sophie, disgustingly cheerful even after a late night clubbing. Or perhaps she hadn't gone to bed yet, Gina thought sleepily.

'Hi, I'm sorry I missed you last night. Do you want to go shopping today?'

'Sure.' Gina sat up and rubbed her eyes, squinting at her watch. 'I have to meet someone at ten, but it shouldn't take long. Shall I come to your place afterwards?'

'Yeah, that'll be fine. I can't wait to tell you about this guy I met last night! He's a professional footballer – or so he says – but he is drop-dead gorgeous...'

'Tell me later, Sophs,' Gina interrupted, with another check on the time. She wanted to wash her hair before going to Jack's. 'I really have to get ready.'

'Oh? Who are you meeting?' Sophie asked curiously. Gina hesitated.

'It's a business meeting.'

'Yeah, right,' Sophie laughed her derision. 'I want all the details later,' she warned.

'Bye, Sophs.' Gina hung up and pushed back the duvet. She opened the window and stuck her head out to check the weather before deciding what to wear, then showered and shampooed her hair, leaving it wrapped in a towel atop her head while she applied make-up.

She knew Jack's house was approximately half-a-mile away but, burdened with the pie and cake, called a taxi to take her there. The driver was less than pleased when told of her destination, but a large tip brought a grudging smile to his face. Feeling unaccountably nervous at the prospect of entering his home – after all they had shared 'The Beeches' all week – she climbed the three steps up to the white-painted front door and, wondering idly who polished the brass fittings to such a high patina, pressed the doorbell.

'Hello, come on in,' Jack smiled a welcome as he pulled

open the door, but he looked exhausted, deep lines of weariness etched around his mouth. He had shaved, she noticed, but seemed to be wearing the same clothes he'd changed into before they left Falworth.

'Have you been working all night?' she asked, concerned.

'Pretty much,' he admitted. 'Come through to the kitchen – I put a fresh pot of coffee on to percolate and it should be ready by now.'

'Mm, it smells delicious,' Gina said, following in his wake and trying to take in her surroundings without seeming overly curious. The hall had plain pale grey walls and a patterned tiled floor with a scattering of rugs. One door was open, the room beyond obviously his study. Another door, disappointingly closed, presumably led to the sitting room. The kitchen he led her to doubled as a dining room and was spacious, with white fittings which Gina felt were too stark for such a big room. However, sunlight streamed in from the patio doors at one end making it more welcoming. Beyond lay a walled garden.

'You're lucky to have a private garden,' Gina commented enviously. She had to share a much smaller communal patch of lawn with the other tenants.

'Mm,' Jack grunted non-committally. High walls to ensure privacy and keep out burglars compared unfavourably to the farm on which he had grown up, or even the spaciousness of 'The Beeches', with its large garden and sea views. He had recently been feeling increasingly stifled by his way of life, never more so than when he had returned home yesterday evening, particularly when his neighbours began playing loud music just as he was getting down to work. But it was rather late to wish he had chosen a different career path!

'I know you're busy,' Gina said quickly, placing her two

packages down on to a working surface and perching on a stool at the breakfast bar, 'but I need to ask you something.'

'Fire away.' Jack poured coffee for them both and pushed a cup over to her, placing milk and sugar near to hand. 'You said you've been discussing my proposals with someone?'

'Yes. Dan Allinson,' she told him. He smiled slightly.

'Excellent choice,' he approved. 'Not many people get his advice for free. Well? Did I pass muster?' he asked, sounding confident that he had.

'Yes, apart from one thing. The same thing that's bothering Gavin and me,' she said. Jack's brows rose.

'And that is?'

'What's in it for you?' she asked bluntly. 'On the face of it, you're working hard for absolutely nothing. No financial gain, anyhow,' she added. Jack sighed.

'I hope you're not going to start that nonsense about Emily again.'

'No,' she shook her head. 'I considered it. I also,' she tried not to blush, 'considered Gavin's notion that Dad wanted to keep the business a family concern by you marrying me. But I don't believe either theory.'

'Thank goodness for that.' Jack poured himself more coffee while he wondered how much to tell her. He couldn't lie to her, yet he couldn't tell her the whole story. Not yet, anyway. 'Gina, I'm in a really awkward position,' he began slowly. 'I made a promise to your father, one which you are now asking me to break. There are some things he didn't want you and Gavin to know about. Will you take it on trust that I have no ulterior motive in building up the business? That I want nothing out of it for myself? I suppose you could say that I'm simply repaying an old debt.'

'That doesn't really tell me anything,' Gina frowned. 'Can't you tell me more about this debt? Not a financial one, but something more personal,' she guessed.

'It's personal,' Jack conceded that much. 'And not actually my debt to repay, but when I heard the company was on the brink of bankruptcy…'

'How did you hear that?' she interrupted.

'I was in Falworth by invitation of the Chamber of Commerce,' he replied, which confirmed what Gavin had told her. 'The president was telling me a bit about the members and your father's name cropped up. I was told he was in poor health and that his company was generally expected to fail. I thought it was a pity – so many old, established family firms have been taken over or gone into liquidation. So, when I was introduced to your father, I offered to help, if I could.' He paused, recalling Peter Bruce's initial reaction.

'And he agreed?' Gina was disbelieving.

'Not at first,' Jack said dryly. 'He was as suspicious as Gavin…but he was a desperate man, Gina,' he continued, 'desperate to safeguard his children's future. He phoned me the next day – I guess he did some checking up on me first – and we arranged to meet. I expect you know what happened next. The idea was for me to be appointed financial director, but it quickly became clear that Gavin wouldn't work with me, so your father presented him with a *fait accompli*.'

'That was so unfair!' she burst out.

'I know,' he nodded. 'It wasn't the way he wanted it, believe me. If he had lived long enough to oversee the company's turnaround, I know he would have changed his will back again, leaving Gavin in control.'

'What are you going to do with your fifty-five per cent of the shares?' she looked deep into his grey eyes. He held her gaze steadily.

'You already know I intend handing over some to Miss Pettit and whoever we appoint as financial director. The remainder I shall sign over to Gavin eventually, apart from a nominal five per cent which will give me the right to attend board meetings and generally keep a watching brief. I'm trusting you not to repeat that to Gavin. Right now, he's co-operating with me because he has no choice. He has to continue to believe that until I feel he's ready to assume overall control,' he said quite sternly. Gina frowned slightly at that, but could see the sense of it. 'Your father trusted me to do what's best for both you and your brother – will you do the same?' Jack asked quietly, hoping desperately that she would. After what seemed an eternity to him, she nodded, albeit rather slowly.

'I have one more question.' Oh no, Jack groaned silently.

'What?'

'Who's Stella Lawson?'

'Stella? Oh, of course, you answered the phone,' he remembered. 'That call was strictly business, I promise. We were involved once, but we broke up over two years ago.'

'Oh,' she digested that in silence for a moment, then said, 'Are you involved with anyone now?' she enquired innocently.

'Only you,' he said simply. Gina was glad she was sitting down.

'Oh,' she said again, then peeped at him from beneath her lashes.

'If you continue looking at me like that, I shall take you on a conducted tour of my house – beginning and ending in the bedroom,' he warned.

'Is that a promise?' Gina asked shakily.

'You bet. But not yet, Gina. This is one situation where I definitely shouldn't mix business with pleasure. There'll be time for us later, all the time in the world,' he hoped. 'Now, get out of here before I change my mind,' he said, with mock ferocity.

'OK,' she agreed, with more reluctance than was lady-like, and got to her feet.

'Don't forget your packages.'

'They're for you. I guessed you'd be too busy to bother cooking. There's a steak-and-kidney pie which just needs heating up and a cake,' she told him rather shyly.

'You're a sweetheart.' He was touched by the thought and dropped a kiss on her mouth, but pulled back before he was tempted to do more.

He showed her out of the house, then returned to the kitchen and removed the lids of the containers. He smiled as he picked a walnut off the top of the cake, then scooped some of the frosting on to his finger and tasted it. Coffee and walnut. She had guessed correctly that it was his favourite. He hadn't bothered with breakfast, apart from lashings of strong coffee, so he cut a huge wedge of the cake to take back to his desk. It was a while before he got down to work though. It was odd, he mused, for years he had assumed that if he did marry – a possibility but not a certainty – it would be to a career woman, someone like Stella Lawson who worked in the City and would understand his work and problems as he would hers. As for children…he had never really considered them except maybe as something one day far in the future. Yet, within a week of meeting Gina Bruce, he now had dreams of a house in the country filled with kids, cats and dogs, and a paddock with ponies for the children as they grew older. And most important of all, a wife far more interested in silk sheets than balance sheets, in making the house a comfortable home, a place to relax, not an extension of the office…he sighed, coming back down to earth with a bump. Before any of those dreams could become a reality, he had to tell her the whole story. And, if he did that, she might hate him. Old sins cast long shadows. The sin wasn't his, but the shadow of it threatened to wreck his future happiness.

The week began on a high note. They arrived back in Falworth on Sunday evening and found a message from Gavin, who had already headed north to Leeds for the Trade Fair, telling them that the weekend with Jerry Carlisle had gone wonderfully well and he had promised to renew his firm's contract with Bruce Casuals.

'That's brilliant!' Gina exclaimed, pleased for the business, but even more pleased because Gavin had proved he could clinch a major deal without Jack looking over his shoulder.

'It certainly is,' Jack agreed. With Taggart and Carlisle back in the fold, things were looking up. 'Does your father keep champagne in the cellar?'

'He does, but I'd prefer fish and chips and a bottle of Coke,' Gina said.

'Sounds good to me,' Jack smiled at her and they wandered, hand-in-hand, down to the sea front where they bought the provisions and ate from the paper wrapping while sitting on the wall and gazing out to sea. It was rather chilly after London, but invigorating.

'It feels good to be back,' Jack said softly. He had almost said 'home'. He glanced at Gina beside him, in jeans and a sweater, her hair blown into disarray by the wind, happily eating takeaway food with her fingers. There was little sign of the spoilt rich kid he had once thought her to be. He noticed she was shivering slightly in the cool breeze and immediately shrugged off his jacket and placed it over her shoulders, keeping his arm around her.

'You'll get cold,' she protested, rather half-heartedly, already snuggling into its warmth.

'No, I won't,' he gave her a smile that warmed her more than his jacket and pulled her closer. They continued eating their supper and swigged Coke from the bottle. If my clients could see me now, they'd defect in droves Jack thought, but didn't care. He felt as if he had spent his adult life amassing a fortune he never had time to enjoy. That was going to change – or so he hoped. He glanced down at Gina. So much depended on her and her reaction to what he must one day, and soon, tell her. Gina caught the intensity of his gaze and her smile faltered.

'What is it?' she whispered. He shook his head, then bent and kissed her, his mouth hard against hers, then the kiss gentled when she opened her mouth beneath his. Her arms went up around his neck to pull him closer and she pressed her body against his. His jacket slipped unheeded to the ground, but neither felt the chill wind any longer.

'I don't suppose you'll care, mate, but someone will nick your wallet if you don't watch out,' said an amused voice behind them.

'Huh?' Jack looked up to see a total stranger holding out his jacket. 'Oh. Right. Thanks,' he took the jacket with a slightly sheepish grin. He looked at the girl beside him. 'So much for not mixing business with pleasure,' he said ruefully. 'Do you want to go for a walk?' he asked briskly. Gina didn't. She wanted to go home and continue what they had been doing, but she sensed he was back in control. What was wrong with mixing business and pleasure anyhow? she wondered, even as she nodded assent and they walked down to the beach. To her disappointment, he turned the conversation to the lunches and fashion show she was organising, and didn't hold her hand or make any physical contact. Back at the house, he bid her and Mary a rather perfunctory goodnight and disappeared to his room.

They drove separately to the factory on Monday morning. Gina found that Petty was bubbling over with enthusiasm for her new role. Ever since Jack had spoken to her about it on Friday afternoon, she had thought of little else. She had several ideas for improvements in administration, ideas she had kept to herself while working for Peter Bruce.

Gina continued with her phone calls, and the list of those attending lunch the following Monday and Tuesday grew longer. If only half were serious about conducting business with Bruce Casuals again, it would be well worth all the effort. At around eleven, she got a call from Gavin in Leeds.

'Hey, well done with Jerry Carlisle,' she congratulated him.

'No sweat,' he said casually. 'I've got two more names for your lunches,' he told her. 'Bill Taggart's coming up trumps – at dinner last night he was telling everyone who'd listen that we're back in business. Mind you, he's also saying what a terrific cook you are, so they might be coming just for a free lunch.'

'Let's steal their car keys and not hand them back until they sign a contract,' Gina suggested. He laughed.

'Worth a try, although I doubt Jack would approve,' he added, but without the rancour with which he normally spoke about him. Perhaps the board meeting, plus a successful weekend, had changed his attitude towards Jack. She certainly hoped so. They chatted for a while longer, then Gavin went off to lunch and Gina decided to tell Jack of the possible new contacts Gavin had already made at the Trade Fair. His office door was ajar and she paused when she heard voices. Then her blood froze.

'…you're being silly, Emily,' Jack was saying gently, 'of course you're more important than Gina…' Gina felt physically sick, yet was rooted to the spot. Luckily, she decided to think later for, if she had run away, she wouldn't have heard the rest. When the buzzing in her ears cleared, she was able to make sense of what Jack was saying.

'…you'll have to accept that. But he chose you, Emily, chose to marry you and have a family with you. It's you he wants to build a future with…'

'But he hardly said two words to me,' Emily sniffed. 'He just asked to speak to Gina.'

'It was probably about the fashion show…stop crying, Emily, and we'll go and ask her…' That galvanised Gina into moving and she ran as silently as she could to the cloakroom. She locked herself into a cubicle and sat down, her heart still pounding. Oh God, the relief! Emily was more important than her to Gavin, not to Jack! She dropped her head into her hands. For one awful, heart-stopping, heart-breaking moment, all her earlier suspicions about Jack and Emily had rushed to the fore…and she hadn't spared a second's thought for Gavin, she realised guiltily. The intense pain had been for herself.

'Oh, I love him,' she whispered out loud. It was scary, yet wonderful too.

She felt absurdly shy about meeting him, as if he would be able to tell from merely looking at her that she had discovered her love for him, so she hurried down to the sewing room out of his way. The girls were using the lunch break to try out their modelling skills, exaggeratedly sashaying along the catwalk to the accompaniment of wolf whistles from some of the drivers who had gathered to watch. Gina made the mistake of admiring a bright yellow-and-red bikini with matching beachrobe which she hadn't seen before.

'Go on, try it on,' one of the girls called out.

'I don't think so,' Gina shook her head smiling.

'It's your size – you can change over there,' Judy Finch pointed to a makeshift screen. Gina didn't want to comply but felt refusal might offend, so shrugged good-naturedly and went behind the screen to change into the swimwear.

If my father could see me now she thought, taking a deep breath before facing the crowd. He would be utterly appalled to see her making an exhibition of herself in front of the workforce. Oh well, she took another deep breath and emerged from behind the screen. The wolf whistles for the boss's daughter were louder than those for the machinists, and the comments were more ribald.

Gina managed not to trip on the steps up to the catwalk and walked along it, forcing herself to go slowly and keeping a smile fixed on her face. She turned, posed for a second, then walked back. Feeling braver as she neared the end of her ordeal, she slipped the short robe off her shoulders and struck a provocative pose. The wolf whistles hit a crescendo when one of the drivers, more daring than the others, snatched the robe from her hand and left her standing in only the skimpy bikini.

'OK guys, remember she is a director,' Jack's voice cut through the hubbub as he strode quickly towards her. Gina scanned his face anxiously, wondering if he was angry. He reached up, put his hands on her waist and lifted her down to floor level, holding her a little longer than was necessary. The workers evidently thought so anyway, because the ribald comments increased. His hands were warm against her skin, but it was the heat in his eyes that made her breath quicken.

'Trust you to stop production,' he said sternly, but his tone of voice belied the desire she saw in his eyes. 'Go home so the rest of us can get some work done,' he ordered, pushing her gently towards the screen. 'OK everyone, show's over,' he called. Gina wriggled out of the bikini and got dressed.

'Judy, do you mind if I keep this?' she asked, wondering if it would be hot enough to be innocently sunbathing when Jack arrived home. Judy nodded.

'It's only a sample. And the colour suits you,' she added.

'Thanks,' Gina smiled.

She left the factory and went home and began working on menus for the lunches, but she couldn't concentrate and so wandered through the house, checking the number of chairs. If the weather stayed fine, there would be enough, for some would undoubtedly prefer to sit outside in deckchairs or sun-loungers. But, if not...she frowned, then remembered seeing an assortment of furniture in the attic and made her way upstairs.

She found what she was looking for – eight matching dining chairs, in heavy mahogany with embroidered upholstered seats and backs. They were Victorian, she thought, and in good condition. Presumably, her mother or grandmother had simply tired of them and replaced them with something new. She wished she had room for them in her flat.

She glanced around, feeling sad that the family antiques would have to be sold. But she didn't have room and Emily preferred modern furniture – she would turn up her nose at the heavy, dark-wood pieces up here. She wandered over to inspect a stack of paintings propped against one wall. Again, they were too large, the frames too ornate for her flat. Most of the subjects were too gloomy for her taste anyway, but she found a smaller watercolour she really liked. She guessed it was also Victorian, of two girls in a garden, one on a swing, the other sitting on the grass, her skirts spread around her as she picked flowers. The details were exquisitely done, Gina thought, taking it over to the window to see better. It needed a professional clean but would look terrific in her bedroom, she decided, and put it to one side. Gavin half-owned it, of course, but she was sure he wouldn't mind if she kept it for herself.

Her curiosity was well and truly piqued now, and she opened, with difficulty, the straps on one of the large leather travelling trunks. It was full of clothes and she began carefully removing them. There were flapper dresses from the twenties, beaded and fringed, in glorious colours. Another dress was of shimmering oyster satin and beneath it were matching shoes, well, dancing slippers she supposed, for they were too insubstantial to be called shoes. She tried to imagine her unsmiling, strict grandmother wearing these clothes, dancing and enjoying herself, but couldn't. Grandmother Bruce had terrified her and Gavin when they were little, constantly complaining that they were out of control and should be banished to the nursery.

She continued delving into the trunk and an evening bag caught her eye. She thought it would look great with a dress she had recently bought, a pale pink strappy number. The bag was pink, lavishly decorated and beaded with a design of flowers and butterflies. Gina drew it out. It seemed vaguely familiar, but she was sure she had never seen her grandmother with it. Perhaps Mum borrowed it, she thought, opening it to remove the tissue paper it had been padded with to keep its shape. Only it wasn't tissue paper. Instead, she drew out a bundle of letters tucked into a folded Valentine's Day card. She glanced idly at one of the envelopes, then stared harder, her brow creasing into a frown. Quickly, she checked the others. They were all addressed to Mrs Vivienne Bruce – and not in her father's handwriting. Her heart beat a little faster. It didn't mean anything! So, Mum kept some letters…and a Valentine's Day card, hidden amongst Grandmother's things. It could have been totally innocent, not letters from a lover…so read one, if you're so sure, urged a voice inside her head.

'No,' Gina said out loud, shoving the letters and card back into the bag and replacing it at the bottom of the trunk. Her pleasure in treasure hunting had disappeared completely and she returned downstairs. She felt grubby after her rummaging in the dusty attic and took a quick shower. Jack would be home soon, she realised, dragging her thoughts back to the present.

The sun was still shining and, with mounting excitement and anticipation, she put on the bikini and matching robe, picked up sunglasses and a book, and went out to the garden. It wasn't really hot enough to sunbathe, so she kept the robe on, settling herself comfortably – and, hopefully, sexily – on one of the loungers.

She gave only a passing thought to Jack's promise to her father, and his insistence on not mixing business with pleasure. To hell with that! It was probably nothing much anyway – her father hadn't even told Gavin the company was in financial trouble. He probably had made a bad decision, lost a lot of money and didn't want her and Gavin to know. She couldn't imagine what else he could have insisted Jack keep quiet about. She didn't care – that was in the past and, if she had read the look in Jack's eyes correctly at lunchtime, they were both more interested in the future.

When she heard car tyres crunching the gravel outside, she quickly took off the robe and lay back on the lounger, one leg raised to display a slim thigh, her eyes closed as if asleep. He would go into the house first, wonder where she was…God, I hope he doesn't just go into the study she thought, beginning to wonder how long she was going to have to lie there, getting goose bumps. And her breathing was so ragged he would never believe she was asleep…where was he?

'I hope you don't mind my coming round here, but no one answered the front door bell,' said a voice that was definitely not Jack's. Gina sat up with a startled cry and grabbed for the robe.

'Oh, it's you.' She recognised Steve Forrest and calmed down a little. 'Sorry, I didn't hear the bell. And Mary's out. What can I do for you?'

'Well, say if my timing's lousy,' Steve began tentatively, 'but I have a couple of kittens in my car. They were abandoned with their mother at the surgery. I was going to take them to the Rescue Centre, but then it occurred to me that you might like to give them a home? I understand perfectly if you feel it's too soon to have another pet,' he finished, aware that he was babbling, but oh boy!, was he glad he had come! Gorgeous when clothed, she was even more stunning in a bikini.

'I'm not sure,' Gina bent to put on her sandals. 'We'll be selling this place soon and I live in a flat in London which isn't suitable for pets. But Mary said she would like a cat when she moves,' she remembered.

'Come and take a look,' Steve invited. 'They need to be with their mum for now, but they could be separated later.'

'Gavin and Emily might take one,' she said, still rather doubtful and feeling as if she were being disloyal to Jasper, but it seemed churlish not to go and take a look when he had gone to trouble to drive over.

She followed him round to the front of the house and bent to peer inside the basket. The mother cat was pure white apart from a smudge of black on her nose, while both kittens were a mixture of black and white.

'Aah, how sweet,' she bent further forward, and her robe fell open and her breasts pushed against the bikini top. Steve forgot the plight of the kittens and stared openly at Gina. Unfortunately, Jack chose that exact moment to drive up to the house. Gina looked up to greet him, but her welcoming smile faded when she noted the grim expression on his face. Now what? Was he angry because she had taken part in the fashion show? Or, cringe-makingly worse, guessed why she was wearing the bikini? Defensively, she wrapped the robe tightly around her – much to Steve's disappointment. Jack's lips thinned even more. It was a bit late for modesty!

'Steve thought I might want to take these kittens,' she stammered.

'How thoughtful,' Jack sneered at the other man. Gina bent to the three cats again. The older gazed up at her anxiously while the kittens sleepily snuggled up to their mother, oblivious to their abandonment.

'Hello, puss,' Gina reached out a gentle hand to the mother cat. 'How could anyone just dump them?' she asked indignantly. Steve shrugged.

'It happens all the time. Some owners can't be bothered to have them neutered, then don't want the result. At least these were left at my surgery – it's the creeps who leave them by the roadside who ought to be strung up,' he finished wrathfully.

'I'll look after them,' Gina decided impulsively, pretty sure she could cajole either Gavin or Mary to take them when they were older.

'I suppose this means you want Jasper's basket back up from the cellar?' Jack asked irritably. He had lugged it down there on Friday so the sight of it wouldn't upset her.

'I can fetch it myself,' she snapped back, then turned a sunny smile on Steve. 'Thank you for thinking of me, that was so sweet.'

'Oh God,' Jack muttered, feeling quite nauseous. Gina ignored him.

'Would you like a drink? Stay until they're settled?' she asked Steve, who accepted with alacrity and carried the three cats into the house. Jack decided he could fetch the stupid basket as well and stomped off to the study, slamming the door behind him. Unfortunately for Jack's temper, he didn't hear Mary come home a few minutes later and join the other two in the kitchen. All he heard was Forrest leaving – finally – an hour later. Only then did he trust himself to emerge from his self-imposed exile in the study, just in time to see Gina – still in the bikini – heading for the stairs. Presumably to put clothes on now her tame vet had gone.

'Wasn't stealing the show at lunchtime enough for you – did you have to steal the stock as well?' he asked coldly.

'I own it, don't I?' she asked haughtily. 'It was only a bit of fun at lunchtime – they'd have thought I was a spoil-sport if I had refused to take part.'

'Really? And what do they think of you now, I wonder?' his lip curled with contempt.

'What's your problem?' she snapped. 'Are you really annoyed about the fashion show or is it because I agreed to take the cats? This *is* my house,' she reminded him.

'Which you keep saying you're going to sell,' Jack

retorted. 'Those cats will have to be uprooted again then, won't they?'

'You think I should have refused to take them? That I'm being selfish?'

'Self-indulgent, certainly. You didn't think it through, did you?'

'Yeah, well, that's me – self-indulgent. Downright spoilt, in fact.'

'You said it,' Jack agreed coldly.

Near to tears, Gina fled upstairs to her room. Once there, she phoned Sophie to pour out her woes.

'I felt such a fool! There I was, draped provocatively across the sun-lounger, waiting to seduce him and the wrong man walked into the garden!' she wailed.

'What did you do? Seduce him instead?' Sophie, safe in London, was laughing her head off.

'No!'

'I would have.'

'You're a trollop.'

'I know. But it has its uses. At least I wouldn't make a pig's ear of seducing a man I fancy rotten. That's the trouble with waiting for Mr Right – when he does come along, you're too inexperienced to know what to do! Would you like me to come down there and show you how to do it?' she offered.

'No, I wouldn't!' Gina howled, and slammed down the phone. She called back later and apologised, but didn't approach Jack. Sophie was right – she simply didn't know how to.

chapter ten

Jack and Gina avoided each as much as possible in the days that followed – no mean feat since they shared both house and workplace. Gina stayed out of his way in the mornings until she knew he had left for work, and spent her time organising the two lunch parties only going to the factory to check on the progress of the redecorating and the fashion shows when she knew Jack had outside appointments.

Petty, loving her new role and responsibilities, actually had both in hand, and Gina knew that, once the catering was over, she wouldn't be needed in Falworth other than to hostess occasional dinner parties for more important clients. With a reluctance she didn't understand, she phoned the estate agent and asked him to put 'The Beeches' on the market.

Jack knew he could probably end the coldness between them with an apology, one she deserved to hear. His anger had cooled quickly, an unreasonable anger borne of jealousy, he readily admitted, but only to himself. There was an end in sight to his time in Falworth – the recruitment agency had already provided names of several promising candidates for the role of financial director, and he had arranged to hold preliminary interviews in London at the end of the week. Gavin could take further interviews himself next week when the candidates could look around the factory and the town. But he held back from approaching Gina. He was hurting enough now, yet if he apologised and they continued getting closer, as before, the time would come when he would have to tell her about the 'debt' he was repaying. And that would probably end the relationship before it had barely begun, and he didn't even want to contemplate the intensity of the pain that would result in. At least, this way, he was able to keep the promise he had made to her father. The knowledge afforded him scant consolation.

'A message for you from Jack,' Mary entered Gina's bedroom on Friday morning. 'He's gone to London, then he's away for the weekend – it's his mother's birthday apparently. He'll be back here on Sunday evening.'

'I can't wait,' Gina muttered.

'Here's his mobile number if you need to contact him,' Mary continued, placing a business card beside her coffee cup. 'And he wants Gavin to call him as soon as he gets back from Leeds.'

'I'm sure he'll be delighted to comply,' Gina smiled sweetly. 'No orders for me?'

'No,' Mary hesitated. 'It's none of my business, but…'

'You're right; it isn't.' Gina pulled the duvet over her head to end the conversation. Sighing, Mary left the room.

Gina apologised later, but didn't hang around to hear any motherly advice. Jack had been out of order, full stop. She didn't know why he had spoken to her way he had, but the possibility that he had guessed her plan to seduce him and had feigned anger to keep her at bay gnawed away at her. Perhaps he was turned off by predatory women, and liked to do the chasing himself. Or perhaps he was simply not turned on by her at all.

She called in at the factory to watch a dress rehearsal of the fashion show, a little apprehensive about it since it had been her idea. But the girls were taking it very seriously, aware of the importance of the buyers' visits and, apart from practising their modelling skills, had volunteered to clean up the notoriously untidy sewing room in their spare time.

'That's great!' Gina applauded loudly as the show came to an end. 'As you know, the buyers will be lunching at the house first, so I guess they'll be here from two-thirty to three o' clock, but Gavin or Mr Dawlish will be escorting them and I'll phone Judy when they're on the way. Any questions? No. Good luck everyone,' she called and left, going in search of Harry, the gardener. He still hadn't forgiven her for bringing in the contract gardeners without consulting him first, and his face took on a martyred expression when he saw her approach. God, did he want her to grovel?

'Harry, I wondered if you would like to work a bit of overtime this weekend up at "The Beeches"?' she asked pleasantly. He considered her for a moment.

'How much?'

'Oh, four or five hours should be enough,' she deliberately misunderstood, and kept her smile in place as he shifted uncomfortably.

'No, I meant how much would you pay,' he muttered.

'Your usual overtime rate,' she suggested. He considered again. Gina stifled a sigh, wishing she had cajoled Gavin into helping her weed the flower-beds and mow the lawns.

'It ought to be double at weekends,' he said finally.

'Fine,' Gina agreed. If Jack objected, she'd pay Harry herself. 'Tomorrow morning at eight o'clock,' she instructed. He was still grumbling about something – really, the words 'pension' and 'redundancy' ought to be spoken more often in his hearing, she thought irritably – when she spotted Gavin's BMW turn in the gates, and she ran over to meet him.

'Hey, the place looks great,' he glanced around as he

got out of the car, stretching after long hours on the road.

'Of course, the decorators hadn't finished before you went to Leeds,' Gina nodded, linking her arm through his as they walked towards the entrance. 'You just missed the fashion show, but I think they'd give you a sneak preview if you asked…what on earth?' she broke off suddenly as Emily, for no reason Gina could see, had burst into tears at the sight of her husband and dashed off to the cloak-room.

'This is all I need,' Gavin sighed.

'Have you two had a row?'

'Not that I know of,' he sighed again. 'I'd better go and ask!'

'Um, I hate to mention this, but Jack wants you to phone him…'

'Can this day get any worse?' he groaned.

'Welcome home,' Gina grinned. 'Jack doesn't know you're back, so go and talk to Emily first,' she suggested. 'I'm going home – talk to you later?'

'Sure,' he nodded, then went off in pursuit of his wife.

By Sunday evening, Gina was a bundle of nerves, both at the prospect of entertaining the people so important to the company and at Jack's imminent return. She and Mary had done as much food preparation as they could in advance and she was waiting for Gavin, who had promised to come over and help shift furniture.

To pass the time, she went up to the attic again and moved the dining chairs she had found, plus several small tables out on to the narrow landing, but decided against attempting to negotiate the steep, narrow stairs with such heavy pieces by herself. She studiously ignored the trunk containing *that* bag with *those* letters hidden inside, and began rummaging instead through boxes containing hers and Gavin's books and toys.

She became so engrossed that she didn't even hear Jack's footsteps on the uncarpeted stairs, and he paused to watch for a moment. She looked about sixteen, sitting cross-legged on the floor, wearing jeans and a white T-shirt, her hair in a ponytail and her unmade-up face smudged with dust. Without intending to, he had actually blurted out the whole story to his mother, then waited miserably for her response, fully expecting her to advise him not to become any more involved than he already was. But she hadn't. She had said to leave the past where it belonged and look to the future, adding that Peter Bruce surely wouldn't have exacted the promise not to tell the twins if he had considered for one moment the possibility that Jack and Gina might fall in love. And, as he was leaving, she had called out, 'Come again soon – and bring Gina to meet me next time!'

'Um,' he cleared his throat. Gina dropped the book she was reading and swivelled round to face him. Warily, he noted. Hardly surprising, but not very heartening. 'Mary said you need some furniture moving downstairs? All this out here presumably,' he added casually.

'Er, yes, but Gavin's coming over to do it,' she said quickly.

'That's OK I might as well do it now I'm here,' he smiled. 'I see you've prepared enough food for an army – it all looks wonderful.'

'Thank you. And I heard the weather forecast earlier – it's supposed to be staying fine for the next couple of days,' she told him, forcing herself not to start fussing with her hair or tugging at her old, shapeless T-shirt. She had purposely not changed or applied make-up in case her theory regarding his dislike of predatory females was correct. How awful if he was dreading the prospect of her hitting on him! But she couldn't look less like a vamp if she tried. He appeared to have enjoyed his weekend, she thought. At least, he certainly seemed far more relaxed than he had before he left for London. Which reminded her…

'How did the interviews for the financial director position go?' she asked, when he returned for a second load of furniture.

'Very well. There were several promising candidates,' he told her. 'I've made a brief report on each for Gavin to read, so he…talk of the devil,' he broke off as Gavin appeared at the bottom of the stairs, but he said it with a smile. 'Gina was just asking about the interviews,' he explained. 'The reports are in my briefcase.'

'I'll go and read them now,' Gavin decided, eyeing the heavy furniture and steep stairs with misgiving.

'No, you won't. You'll give me a hand with these!' Jack retorted. To Gina's amazement and pleasure, Gavin laughed.

'OK, I can see it needs some real muscle,' he mocked, but good-naturedly, as he climbed the stairs and began to help. Gina did the important task of telling the two men where to place the various items downstairs, then prepared coffee for all of them while Gavin and Jack discussed the interviewees.

'Why didn't Emily come – is she still in a huff?' Gina asked idly.

'No, she just decided to stay at home,' was all Gavin said, but Gina's intuition sprang into life. Before her brain had finished the thought, her mouth was in use.

'She's pregnant!' she exclaimed.

'How do you know?' Gavin said in disgust. Em would never believe he hadn't spilled the beans. Jack stared at

Gina, one brow raised questioningly. She grinned, shrugging.

'I'm right, aren't I?'

'Yes, but please don't say anything, not even to Em. She miscarried at ten weeks last time and she doesn't want anyone to know until she's safely past that,' he explained.

'We'll pretend we don't know,' Gina assured him. Jack nodded assent, then proffered a handshake.

'Congratulations,' he said warmly.

'Thanks,' Gavin nodded.

'How long have you known?' Gina asked.

'About an hour longer than you have!' Gavin told her ruefully. 'Emily's known for a couple of weeks, but she wasn't going to tell me in case...well, you know.'

'She's kept it to herself? That's why she's been so...emotional,' Gina hastily substituted for 'moody'.

'Mm, I was getting worried. I knew there was something on her mind...well, I'd better get back,' he stood up. 'I'll take these reports with me,' he added to Jack.

'Sure; I think it would be worthwhile seeing them all.' Jack accompanied him out and Gina sat back to finish her coffee, expecting Jack to either go upstairs or into the study.

But he returned to the drawing room and poured himself a glass of wine before sitting beside her. Gina began to wish she had gone easy on the scruffy, as-nature-intended look.

'One of the applicants wants to move out of London because his wife is pregnant,' he told her. 'Maybe that's an omen.'

'I just hope it all goes well this time,' Gina gnawed her lower lip anxiously.

'Mm. How about you? Do you want to have kids one day?' he asked, oh so casually. He hoped. Gina shrugged carelessly. If she said 'yes' he'd probably run for the hills!

'I've never really thought about it. Ask me again when I've been an auntie for a while!' she grinned.

'I might just do that,' Jack said softly, and turned to look at her. Gina's mouth went dry and her heart began pounding so heavily she was sure he must hear it. This wasn't fair! Half the time he behaved as if he were in love with her or at least fancied her rotten, the other half as if she were something the cat had dragged in...cats! A safe topic of conversation!

'The kittens can climb the stairs now,' she told him. They had been struggling only days before, clawing at the carpet in desperate and futile attempts to explore upstairs.

'Does that mean I have to watch what I'm treading in upstairs as well as down?' Jack asked dryly, and she giggled.

'They're very good – we've only had one accident this weekend.'

'I suppose your love-struck vet has been round to check on them?' he asked next.

'He...' Gina stopped. Had he sounded the tiniest bit jealous? 'Love-struck?' she repeated.

'Come off it, Gina, he can't take his eyes off you,' Jack said roughly. 'And you don't exactly discourage him, do you? Flaunting your...assets when he brought the damned kittens here.'

'Flaunting?...I didn't know he was coming,' she protested.

'Really? It was a bit cold for sunbathing that day I'd have thought,' he said caustically. Gina bit her lip in indecision then, praying that whoever said honesty was the best policy had got it right, plunged in.

'It was too cold,' she agreed. 'But I wasn't expecting Steve Forrest to walk into the garden. I was expecting you,' she admitted softly. That was Jack's undoing and, with a groan, he pulled her into his arms and kissed her with all the pent-up desire and frustration that had been building up in him since he had first laid eyes on her.

Gina responded hungrily, and gasped with pleasure as his hands sought naked skin beneath her T-shirt and when he cupped her breast and teased the already erect nipple, she moaned deep in her throat and began tugging at the buttons on his shirt, needing to feel his bare skin against her own.

'Not here,' Jack said hoarsely, finally heeding the one coherent thought in his head, namely that they weren't alone in the house. He pulled away a little and cupped her face in his hands. 'Come to bed with me?' he asked softly. Gina nodded mutely, although she wasn't sure she still had the ability to walk, never mind climb stairs. But with his strong arm around her waist, she managed to do both, quite quickly in fact, and when he closed his bedroom door behind them, she went unhesitatingly into his arms.

They had both been waiting too long for this to happen, and clothes were shed in mere seconds, then Jack drew her down to the bed. He forced himself to slow down and gazed his fill at her body, so sleek and perfect, her breasts a jutting temptation to be kissed. He bent his head to each rosy nipple in turn, becoming ever more aroused by Gina's soft cries of delight urging him on.

When his hand moved to between her thighs, she arched against him, already slick with desire. He positioned himself between her legs and gazed down into her beautiful brown eyes, wanting to watch the expression on her face as he slowly eased into her.

She moved her hips against him, wanting, needing him to be deeper within her. She caught his rhythm and they moved as one, Jack fighting for control. She was so hot, tight and welcoming that he was afraid he would climax too soon. But then he felt her approaching orgasm, felt her muscles contract around him and gave himself up to the most exquisite pleasure he had ever known.

'Wow,' was all Gina could say when her breathing eventually slowed sufficiently for her to speak at all.

'Wow,' Jack agreed with a smile, and pulled a sheet over their sweat-slicked bodies. He cradled her to him and they lay sleepily together, content just to hold each other close. But not for long. A tender kiss rekindled desire and they enjoyed long, drugging kisses, slow caressing explorations that banished post-coital drowsiness.

Jack turned on to his back and lifted Gina on top of him, his hands on her hips guiding her movements. She caught her breath as his fullness embedded itself deep within her, and felt herself begin to spiral out of control again. When it was over, she collapsed on to his chest, panting for breath. And, this time, when he turned her on to her side and held her within his strong embrace, she did fall asleep. Jack watched her for a long time, his heart filled with love – and with dread of what he had to tell her. And Gavin. Tuesday evening, he decided, after all the buyers had left. He would tell them both then, hopefully, take Gina away for a few days holiday…and propose. He knew without a shadow of a doubt that he wanted her to be his wife. If only she understood…

If Mary knew that Gina hadn't spent the night in her own bed, she didn't mention it. Gina was too happy to care if she had. Jack had left early for the factory but he and Gavin were coming back in time to greet the guests.

The weather forecaster had got it right. Sun shone from a cloudless sky and she set out the garden furniture, then prepared the buffet while Mary tidied the house. Most of the food was cold, laid out on the dining room table under Clingfilm. There were also individual pizzas and quiches to be served hot, and two pans of home-made soup on the stove ready to be reheated. Plates, napkins and cutlery were piled ready for use, and bottles of wine had been brought up from the cellar.

Gavin arrived first, closely followed by Jack. Gina, unsure of Gavin's reaction to her new relationship with Jack, stayed in the kitchen, emerging only when the guests began to arrive. She was too busy then to be nervous, chatting and ensuring everyone had food and drink, and avoiding the clutches of Simon Brown, aka trifle-with-cat-hair man.

'If he pinches me one more time, I'm going to hit him,' she threatened to Gavin. 'If I want my backside black and blue, I'll go to Italy and get a decent suntan at the same time!'

'Ask Jack to toss him over the edge of the cliff,' he suggested blandly.

'Not before he signs a contract...' She stopped, realising what he had said. Since when had he abdicated from his self-appointed role as defender of her virtue? She turned towards him sharply and found him regarding her quizzically. She sighed, intuition worked both ways.

'You're both trying too hard not to look at each other – and failing miserably,' he told her. 'Be careful, Gina.'

'That's rich, coming from a guy who had a shotgun wedding!' she retorted.

'Ouch. Below the belt,' he complained. 'Are you sure you know what you're getting into?'

'I've never been more sure of anything,' she said simply. He looked at her hard, then nodded.

'I just hope he isn't playing games,' he said grimly.

'He isn't,' she assured him quickly. 'I asked him about

his reason for helping the business and he told me he's repaying some sort of debt. But it's something Dad made him promise not to tell us about, so I didn't press him for details. I trust him. And Dan Allinson vouched for him,' she added, which was almost true. Gavin considered that for a moment, then nodded again, still not totally convinced.

'I'd better go back in and mingle. See you later.'

'OK.' Gina expelled a sigh of relief. That had gone better than she could have hoped, and once Jack signed over the bulk of his shares to Gavin, there would be no reason for any animosity at all.

Shortly after two, the guests drifted off towards the factory and a conducted tour culminating in the fashion show. Gina didn't envy the girls at all and hoped Simon had more sense than to get too close – she couldn't imagine the machinists tolerating his groping hands. There was likely to be swift retaliation in the form of a well-aimed knee!

'God, what a mess.' She surveyed the kitchen in dismay.

'You should see the dining room,' Mary told her, walking past with a tray laden with used crockery.

'And we have it all to do again tomorrow!' Gina reminded her. She only hoped it would prove worthwhile and result in badly needed new orders.

The chaos was sorted quite quickly. The dishwasher and washing machine hummed, glassware washed and polished by hand. The food was put away and more taken from the freezer for the next day's lunch. The drawing room and dining room were vacuumed and dusted, kitchen tidied, cats rescued from the utility room and allowed free run of the house and garden again.

By four-thirty they had finished, and Gina decided to bathe and change before Jack came home. She told Mary to take a break too, and they both retired upstairs. As Gina lay in a hot bubble bath, tiredness waned and excitement grew.

Jack left the factory as early as he could, eager to be alone with Gina. There was no sign of her when he arrived home though, and he guessed she was taking a shower. By coincidence, he needed one too! Ignoring his own bathroom, he made his way to Gina's and tapped lightly on the door.

'Yes?' Gina guessed – hoped – it was Jack and quickly whipped off the unflattering shower cap as he opened the door.

'Room for two?' Jack decided a bath was preferable to a shower, after all. He rid himself of his clothes in a trice and stepped into the bath behind her, one long leg stretched either side of her. She leaned back against his chest and his hands moved round to cup her breasts then moved lower to part her thighs. The sensation wrought by his clever fingers were intensified by the warm soapy water and she squirmed against his hands, sending a tidal wave over the side of the bath, soaking the carpet and his discarded clothes.

'Gina?' Mary called suddenly, startling them both.

Gina scrambled out of the bath and wrapped herself in a towel before opening the door a crack. 'I'm in the bath.'

'Oh, sorry. I've decided to go to the cinema.'

'Good. I thought I'd have to bribe her with a tenner to go out,' Jack said. Gina flapped a hand at him to be quiet.

'OK,' she called back. 'See you tomorrow.' She turned back to Jack and grinned. 'We've got the house to ourselves!'

'Do you want to go out this evening?' he asked, hoping she would say 'no'.

'No.'

'That's what I like – a cheap date,' he approved.

'Oh! You…' Gina picked up a sponge and squeezed soapy water over his head.

'I've got soap in my eyes,' he complained, blindly reaching out for a towel and – by coincidence, honest! – snatched the one covering Gina's body.

'You cheated,' she accused, trying not too hard to avoid being pulled back into the bath. 'You need a shave,' she murmured a long time later.

'Sorry.' Jack rubbed his stubbled cheeks, then touched the reddening marks on her face and breasts. He clambered out of the bath and wrapped a towel around his waist. 'I'll go and do it now.' He paused. 'Will you wear that negligee you were wearing the first morning I kissed you?' he asked, his eyes dark with remembered desire.

'Yes,' Gina smiled. 'Two minutes,' she promised.

'My place, or yours?' he nodded towards her bedroom door.

'Yours,' she decided promptly. She was half-afraid her father's ghost would appear if she made love in the bedroom she'd had since childhood.

That night was another of intense, urgent coupling, followed by exquisite tenderness and gentle, slow explorations that culminated in more bouts of love-making until, sated, they fell deeply asleep in each other's arms.

Tuesday began as Monday had, with frantic food preparation and setting out of garden furniture, followed by a nervous wait until the first guests arrived. At least there were no gropers today, Gina thought.

'It seems to be going well,' she said to Jack at one point, then her expression changed. 'Oh no, a gatecrasher.'

'Where?' Jack looked round, half-expecting to see a leather-clad Hell's Angel. Instead, Gina pointed to a little old lady clutching a large handbag and wearing a bemused expression.

'Mrs Martin. She used to live next door. She's in a nursing home now but she escapes occasionally. I guess she saw all the cars outside and decided to join the party. She's harmless – give her a sherry and some food, will you? I'll phone the nursing home when I have a minute.'

'OK.' Jack did as she suggested and steered the old lady to a chair in a corner.

'Thank you,' she peered at him uncertainly. 'You're not Gavin.'

'No. My name's Jack Dawlish,' he told her, and she nodded and began eating. She stayed in her corner, unnoticed by most, and Gina ensured she had regular refills of food and sherry to keep her quiet. After Jack and Gavin had accompanied the guests to the factory, Gina phoned the nursing home before beginning the task of clearing up, and was told they would send someone to collect Mrs Martin as soon as they could.

'Let me help dear,' Mrs Martin offered, wandering in to the kitchen.

'Sure,' Gina handed her a tea towel and left her to it.

'Lovely party, lots of men!' Mrs Martin beamed. 'That handsome young man – did he say his name's Dawlish?'

'That's right. Jack Dawlish,' Gina said, just for the pleasure of saying it out loud.

'Not Jack,' Mrs Martin frowned. 'Andrew. Randy Andy – that's what Vivienne used to call him,' she chortled. Gina felt a frisson of apprehension feather her spine.

'His name's Jack,' she said firmly. 'You've forgotten that my mother died thirteen years ago.'

'I know that,' Mrs Martin said huffily. 'I'm not talking about this new chap. I'm telling you about Andrew

Dawlish – he was the one Vivienne was running off with the night she died.'

'You're talking rubbish!' Gina rounded on her furiously, itching to slap her silly, senile face.

'No, I'm not. I was Vivienne's alibi often enough…' her face crumpled suddenly. 'Oh dear. I promised Peter I would never tell a soul…don't tell him, Gina.' She clutched at Gina's hand, but she jerked away and ran upstairs, then up the next flight to the attic. Breathing heavily, she flung open the trunk and rummaged for the bag she had found. Her hands were shaking. In fact, her entire body was trembling as she wrenched it open and grabbed the bundle of envelopes. The postmark on one leaped out at her – Ross-on-Wye. The Wye valley, where Jack grew up…and Andrew? She remembered at the reading of the will…James Andrew Dawlish. She pulled out one of the letters. 'My darling Vivienne,' she read, then turned it over to see the signature. Andrew!

'Oh no, oh my God,' she whispered. Clutching the letters, she raced downstairs and grabbed her car keys. She hit the gatepost as she reversed out of the drive and that jolted her, literally, into taking more care and she concentrated only on driving safely as she headed for the factory.

'Where's Jack?' she demanded of Emily, as she hurtled in to the reception area.

'Still with Mr Carson, I think…'

'Where?'

'In his office…' Gina turned and ran, colliding with Gavin at the top of the stairs.

'Steady on, whatever's wrong?' He grabbed her shoulders, noting her pale face and haunted expression. Wordlessly, Gina thrust the letters at him. He glanced at them, puzzled.

'Mum. And Jack's father,' she managed.

'Come into my office.' Gavin led her inside and sat her down, more concerned with her than the letters. Jack, escorting Mr Carson – fortunately the last of the buyers to leave – off the premises, did a double take as he passed Gavin's office. He asked Miss Pettit to accompany Mr Carson out and hurried back to see what was going on.

'What…?' He stopped, recognising the handwriting on the envelopes and closed his eyes in despair. 'I was going to tell you tonight,' he said, but even to his own ears it sounded lame. Gavin straightened and faced him, his fists balled at his sides.

'Outside!' he hissed.

'Not now, Gavin.' Jack sighed and pushed past him. 'Gina?' he said softly. She didn't, couldn't, look at him.

'You should have told me before…before…' she whispered. Gavin laughed harshly.

'He wouldn't have got what he wanted then, would he? What's this all about, Dawlish? Revenge? Payback time?'

'You're completely wrong,' Jack shook his head. 'I've been working my butt off trying to make amends for the damage my father caused your family,' he said. 'Gina? You have to believe me,' he said urgently. She barely heard him. Ever since Sunday evening, she had been dreaming of a white wedding, of having Jack's mother in her life even…oh, God, of bringing about a reconciliation between him and his father. She shuddered, afraid she was about to be sick.

'I need some air,' she got to her feet.

'Very well,' Jack decided to give her some time alone, while he dealt with Gavin. 'But you're not driving anywhere,' he said firmly, taking her bag from her and removing the car keys before handing it back. Gina said nothing, but left the room and, icily calm now, walked steadily to Petty's desk and removed the spare set before heading out to the car park.

'Right…' Jack turned back to Gavin, but found himself on the receiving end of his fist, which made him stagger back. 'Grow up, Gavin!' he knocked his arm aside as he took another swing. 'If you bothered to talk to the accountant or bank manager occasionally, you'd know that I have personally guaranteed the company's loans! If Bruce Casuals goes under, I stand to lose an awful lot of money, not to mention my reputation of knowing a good business deal when I see one! Does that really sound like an act of revenge?' he demanded.

'Why do you care about the company?' Gavin sneered, not convinced.

'My father was partly responsible for your mother's death, and that was when your father began to lose his grip on the business. It only survived as long as it did because he kept pumping his personal fortune into it. If I hadn't stepped in, you'd be bankrupt,' Jack said flatly. 'I wanted to make amends for my father's actions. It was meant to be a purely business arrangement. But not now. I love Gina and I intend to marry her, even though it means having you as a brother-in-law,' he added. 'Now get out of my way!' he gritted. Gavin was so taken aback by the declaration that he made no move to stop Jack going after Gina, but trailed after him, as concerned for her as Jack.

Their concern grew when they couldn't find her.

'Emily, have you seen Gina?' Jack asked urgently.

'I think she left,' she told him, looking at Gavin. 'What's going on?'

'How? I've got her car keys.' Jack ignored her question.

'I expect she took the spare set,' Gavin muttered.

'What?' Jack rounded on him. 'You idiot! Do you want

to see history repeat itself?' he blazed, running out to his own car. Gavin's face was ashen. He had been so pleased to see Gina getting one over on Jack, that he hadn't considered the possible consequences.

'Gavin!' Emily's hurt voice stopped him as he began to run after Jack, and he turned to her.

'Get someone to cover for you – we'll talk in the car,' he said.

Jack's car was already at 'The Beeches' when Gavin pulled up outside. There was no sign of the Volvo. Jack and Mary turned quickly as the new arrivals entered, but their faces fell when they saw it wasn't Gina.

'She's been here, but she left again,' Jack said quickly. 'And she hasn't gone to the flat – Mary says she packed a case. Where would she go, Gavin?'

'I don't know,' he shook his head.

'Think, man! We have to find her…' He swallowed, fighting for control, his fear for her plain to see. Gavin no longer doubted that Jack loved her.

'Did she phone anyone? Press redial!' He dashed to the phone but Jack got there before him, pressed the button and prayed that she had called a friend, or booked into a hotel. 'Hello? My name's Jack Dawlish…'

'Yes, Jack, I do recognise your voice,' said his mother, sounding bemused. For a moment, he was struck dumb.

'Gina's just phoned you.'

'Gina? No, the only call this afternoon has been from a Miss Brewster, asking if I had a room vacant for tonight…that was Gina Bruce?'

'Yes, I'm sure it was…she found some letters, she's upset. I should catch up with her on the road, but if she does arrive, look after her for me,' he pleaded.

'Of course I will,' she promised. Jack hung up and turned to Gavin. 'I know where she's heading – can you stay here in case she changes her mind or tries to talk to you? Call me on my mobile if you hear anything.'

'Yes, get going,' Gavin pushed him towards the door. Emily ran after them.

'Jack, if it's any consolation, she asked to speak to you when she came to the factory, not Gavin,' she told him. He paused, then nodded and smiled slightly.

Jack pushed the Jag to its limits as soon as he was on the motorway, dreading seeing the wreck of the Volvo. She could only have a twenty-minute lead. He almost missed it, had to slam on his brakes and enter the service area via the exit, thus earning himself the ire of departing travellers. As if he cared.

He ran over to where Gina was still sitting in the Volvo, slumped over the steering wheel and sobbing her heart out. Jack wrenched open the passenger door and slipped inside, pulling her into his arms.

'Stop crying, please, I love you,' he murmured over and over, and told her what he had already told Gavin earlier. 'Please, darling, you're breaking my heart. I love you so much and we're going to get married and have loads of kids and be so happy together. The past doesn't matter, not if we don't let it,' he said urgently. Eventually, she stopped crying and sniffed, rubbing her hand across her face like a child.

'It's all spoiled now,' she whispered.

'No, it is not,' he said firmly. 'Why were you going to see my mother?'

'I don't know…I wanted to meet her…to say sorry…'

'You have nothing to apologise for. But she does want to meet you – I told her all about you.'

'She must hate me…'

'Of course she doesn't.'

'But, my mum…'

'You're not responsible for what your mother did when you were ten-years-old. Don't you want to know what I told her about you?'

'That I'm spoilt…'

'No. That you're beautiful and sexy, and funny and loyal…and that I'm hopelessly in love with you and want desperately to marry you.'

'But,' she looked at him, 'how can we? Your father…' she shuddered. 'I don't ever want to meet him.'

'You won't have to, I promise,' he said firmly. 'He's made a career out of damaging other people's lives and I am heartily glad he lives on the other side of the world. I will never let him come anywhere near you,' he said earnestly. 'And I am so sorry I didn't explain all this to you before, but I was afraid of your reaction,' he continued.

'Was that the promise you made to Dad? Not to tell Gavin and me?'

'Yes, he didn't want you to know about the affair. He knew how much you both loved her and didn't want to tarnish her memory.' He paused, then said, 'Actually, that's why he sent you to boarding school – he was afraid the truth might come out and the kids at the school in Falworth would taunt you with it.'

'But he separated us.' That still hurt, even after thirteen years.

'I know. He didn't want to but…'

'Go on,' she urged when he hesitated.

'Gavin became very withdrawn, didn't he? He wouldn't speak to anyone but you, wouldn't even answer a direct question – you spoke for him. Your father took medical advice and was told Gavin would recover quicker in a new environment and without you to hide behind.'

'Oh.' Gina digested that for a moment. 'I don't know

how I feel about either of my parents now. My mum…'

'…is still the loving mother you remember her to be,' Jack said gently. 'Whatever happened in the marriage takes nothing away from the love she had for her children. Talking of marriage, I haven't had your answer yet.' He cupped her chin in his hand and gazed into her eyes. 'Will you marry me? Please?' It seemed an eternity to him, but was in fact only a few seconds before she flung herself into his arms.

'Yes, oh yes!' Her voice was muffled against his chest, then she lifted her face for his kiss and felt the pain and uncertainty melt away. Eventually, they pulled apart and smiled shakily.

'Shall we go home?' he asked softly and she nodded. 'Leave the Volvo and drive back with me.'

'I'm OK to drive now,' she told him.

'I know you are. But I want you with me. Always,' he said simply.

'Always,' she repeated. Her eyes no longer shimmered with tears, but were filled with joy and happiness as he took her hand in his and they walked together towards their future.

Why not start a new romance today with Heartline Books. We will send you an exciting Heartline romance ABSOLUTELY FREE. You can then discover the benefits of our home delivery service: Heartline Books Direct.

Each month, before they reach the shops, you will receive four brand new titles, delivered directly to your door.

All you need to do is to fill in your details opposite – and return them to us at the address below.

Please send me my free book:

Name (IN BLOCK CAPITALS)

_____

Address (IN BLOCK CAPITALS)

_____

_____

_____

_____   Postcode _____

Freepost Address:
HEARTLINE BOOKS
PO Box 400
Swindon SN2 6EJ

We may use this information to send you offers from ourselves or
selected companies, which may be of interest to you.

If you do not wish to receive further offers
from Heartline Books, please tick this box ☐

If you do not wish to receive further offers
from other companies, please tick this box ☐

Once you receive your free book, unless we hear from you otherwise,
within fourteen days, we will be sending you four exciting new romantic
novels at a price of £3.99 each, plus £1 p&p. Thereafter, each time you
buy our books, we will send you a further pack of four titles.

You can cancel at any time! You have no obligation to ever buy a
single book.

Heartline Books –
romance at its best!

What do you think of this month's selection?

As we are determined to continue to offer you books which are up to the high standard we know you expect from Heartline, we need you to tell us about *your* reading likes and dislikes. So can we please ask you to spare a few moments to fill in the questionnaire on the following pages and send it back to us? And don't be shy – if you wish to send in a form for each title you have read this month, we'll be delighted to hear from you!

Questionnaire

Please tick the boxes to indicate your answers:

1   Did you enjoy reading this Heartline book?

    Title of book: _____

    A lot   ☐
    A little   ☐
    Not at all   ☐

2   What did you particularly like about this book?

    Believable characters   ☐
    Easy to read   ☐
    Enjoyable locations   ☐
    Interesting story   ☐
    Good value for money   ☐
    Favourite author   ☐
    Modern setting   ☐

3   If you didn't like this book, can you please tell us why?

_____

_____

4 Would you buy more Heartline Books each month if they were available?

Yes ☐

No – four is enough ☐

5 What other kinds of books do you enjoy reading?

Historical fiction ☐

Puzzle books ☐

Crime/Detective fiction ☐

Non-fiction ☐

Cookery books ☐

Other _____

_____

6 Which magazines and/or newspapers do you read regularly?

a) _____

b) _____

c) _____

d) _____

And now a bit about you:

Name _____

Address _____

_____

_____ Postcode _____

Thank you so much for completing this questionnaire.
Now just tear it out and send it in an envelope to:

HEARTLINE BOOKS
PO Box 400
Swindon SN2 6EJ

(and if you don't want to spoil this book, please feel free
to write to us at the above address with your comments
and opinions.)

Ref: PWF

Have you missed any of the following books:

Complete your collection by ringing the Heartline Hotline on 0845 6000504, visiting our website www.heartlinebooks.com or writing to us at Heartline Books, PO Box 400, Swindon SN2 6EJ